Squashed

Squashed

Joan Bauer

Delacorte Press

Published by
Delacorte Press
Bantam Doubleday Dell Publishing Group, Inc.
1540 Broadway
New York, New York 10036

Library of Congress Cataloging in Publication Data

Bauer, Joan [date of birth]
    Squashed / Joan Bauer.
       p.   cm.
    Summary: As a sixteen-year-old pursues her two goals—growing the biggest pumpkin in Iowa and losing twenty pounds herself—she strengthens her relationship with her father and meets a young man with interests similar to her own.
    ISBN 0-385-30793-4
    [1. Pumpkin—Fiction.   2. Country life—Fiction.]   I. Title.
PZ7.B32615Sq 1992
[Fic]—dc20
                                    91-44905
                                      CIP
                                      AC

Manufactured in the United States of America

October 1992

10 9 8 7 6 5

BVG

For Evan, my squash partner

Squashed

Chapter One

I was **preparing my secret** booster solution of one
part buttermilk, two parts Orange Crush, and
about to inject it into the thick stem of my world-class
Big Max—technically a variety of squash, but often the
winner in giant pumpkin contests. I called him Max for
short. He was the biggest squash I had ever grown—
107 inches wide around his middle—which put him over
300 pounds, approximately. Awesome was the only
word for it, especially since this was only August. We
had forty-six days to go until the Rock River Pumpkin
Weigh-In and Harvest Fair, where I, at sixteen years
of age, am *the only teenager ever* to enter the adult
growing division. I was facing heavy competition for
the blue ribbon from Cyril Pool, four-time Weigh-In
champ and a deeply despicable person. If I didn't win I
was sure I'd die, which was why I couldn't bother with
anything else right now.

I stirred my booster solution to get it good and
frothy and let the long tube attached to Max's stem

carry the mixture to his core. This would, hopefully, make him more intensely mammoth, which is what growing giant pumpkins is all about. That, and absolute courage.

I patted Max, who gurgled happily, and fixed thoughts of victory in my mind. I could see myself acing the blue ribbon from Cyril Pool's grungy hands— bowing to the crowd, who roared their support. Standing proudly as Mrs. McKenna pinned the blue ribbon on *me*. Waving to the press, saying, "It was nothing, really." Being carried on my classmates' shoulders across Founders' Square, playing it real humble.

My cousin Richard threw his baseball into a nearby bushel basket. Richard's baseball usually showed up before he did, indoors or out. He ran to get it and delivered the news.

"Cyril Pool figures his pumpkin weighs four hundred pounds, Ellie," he said. "I swear."

"Cyril Pool's full of it," I spat back.

"Well, you don't have to believe me," Richard yelled, "but I was there and I saw them measure it with the chart."

"They probably rigged the chart," I said, stroking Max but dying inside. The "chart" was from the World Pumpkin Federation and estimated a pumpkin's weight by its size. I didn't think rigging the chart was possible, but if anyone was low enough to try, it was Cyril.

Richard was not happy about bringing me the news. He threw his baseball high in the air away from him and ran to catch it like he did catching pop flies in the outfield. Richard was a partial baseball star and working hard to become famous.

"Anything could happen," he said. "It's only August."

I hated August because it was hot and muggy and keeping a pumpkin safe took some doing. In August a Big Max could turn on you, just sit there, and that's all I needed. I'd gained seven pounds already from all the butterscotch swirl ice cream I ate while worrying.

"I thought you'd want to know," Richard said, waiting.

"We're having smoked pork chops with sweet corn," I offered. Richard's face went rapturous.

Richard ate with us about four nights a week because his mother (my aunt Peg) had been in a car accident and couldn't get around too well yet and fixed mostly TV dinners. Richard didn't complain about it around me because my mother had died in a car crash when I was eight. My father says that's why I'm twenty pounds overweight.

I am, quite possibly, one of Iowa's great cooks. Everybody says so. Richard would rather eat my cooking than do anything except play baseball, and since we were cousins, it all worked out. I make the best desserts in all of Rock River High, and Richard eats them. I swirl the frosting on top of the cakes and decorate them with walnuts and pecans. Once I made frosting out of powdered sugar and orange juice and put a spiral of orange slices on top of a cake that was packed with rum-soaked raisins. Nobody could believe the taste. I'm starting my diet tomorrow.

My father is anxious for me to lose weight. He says being overweight keeps me from discovering my true potential. He talks that way because he is a motivational specialist who gets paid to remake people's lives. He gives speeches to companies and groups who need to be motivated and can't seem to do it on their own. He makes tapes on success. He's very happy doing this and has changed a lot of people's lives in the greater Des Moines area and made them become more interesting, productive, and self-sustaining. Dad says if I stop being so stubborn he can do that with me.

Dad specializes in difficult cases, which is why he holds out hope for me. His most famous pupil was Warren Bowler, a rotten accountant who got turned around by Dad's tape series, *Self-Imaging III*. Mr. Bowler believed in himself so much after listening to Dad's tapes that he ran for treasurer of Rock River and *won*. Dad respected Mr. Bowler's spunk but didn't vote for him. Only God could turn Mr. Bowler into a decent accountant, Dad said, and God had easier things to work on, like world peace. Mr. Bowler was kicked out of office eventually, but managed to leave with his head high, a tribute to motivational therapy.

Dad believes in having Important Life Goals (he says, "A life without goals is a life without direction") and is constantly writing his personal goals down on pads: Finding More Clients, Beating Insomnia, Running Seven Miles in Under Forty Minutes, Learning Japanese. I happen to think this is fine for some people, but for me, I have two goals right now. That's all I can handle, and I don't have to write them down. I want to grow the biggest pumpkin in Iowa and win the ribbon at the Harvest Fair, and I want to lose these stupid twenty pounds once and for all.

I've lost the weight, you understand, probably ten, eleven times, I just keep putting it back. As for pumpkin growing, Richard's news about Cyril's squash was bad, very bad. Cyril always wins because he's thirty-five and doesn't have anything else to do except booster his squashes. I always come in second because I have to take care of the house, cook, go to school, *and* be a great pumpkin expert. We've tried housekeepers before but they could never cook as well as me.

Dad says he wouldn't give up my dinners for anything and gives me a good chunk extra each week in allowance. My mother was a superior cook, and I make some of her recipes. Her specialty was sweet sausage ragout with homemade noodles. I used to help her roll out the noodle dough and cut the strips myself. Mother taught me a lot about cooking. Whenever I make Mother's recipes I feel close to her, like she's part of the ingredients. Dad gets real quiet and always has thirds.

Richard went home to tell his mother he was staying for dinner, and that's when I started to cry. I really hate surprises, emotional or otherwise, and like most growers try to take the long view. I knew I was crying about Cyril's pumpkin and how life was unfair and I was probably going to come in second again. Miss Runner-Up. Miss Congeniality. I saw myself standing next to Cyril, who always wore all his ribbons pinned on his shirt when he accepted another one. I was smiling and congratulating him and being a big sport, thinking a plague of locusts would fix him good. I was sixteen years old and had never kissed a boy or had a date. I wanted to be pretty, but my hair was brown and boring and hung down my back like yarn. I had great skin, but twenty pounds too much of it. I wanted to be noticed and kept getting ignored. I'd given Max the best months of my life, but now my world-class pumpkin seemed second-rate. My life was passing in front of my eyes, and it was pudgy.

The last time I got this way, Richard reminded me of a few things. "You won the Rock River Young Growers' Competition three times," he said. Which was absolutely true and a great honor, but that, I reminded him, was for young people.

"You are a young person," Richard pointed out.

"But I'm good enough to compete with adults. How am I going to get better if I keep entering contests I already know I can win?" Richard nodded at this and asked when dinner would be ready.

I had stopped crying now and dusted a piece of lint off of Max, ashamed I had doubted him. It was, after all, only August. Forty-six days to go. Anything could happen, as we say in the growing biz.

I grew giant pumpkins because I liked battle, and growing one was an everyday fight. You had to be in it for the long haul. Rain, frost, bugs, and fungus could strike at any time and stop you dead. Only certain growers are cut out to handle this pressure—tough people of steel who can stand against the odds. Richard says giant-pumpkin growers are the spawning salmon of agriculture, since only the strongest make it up-stream each year for anything worth mentioning.

Not all vegetables are this draining. Lettuce doesn't bring heartache. Turnips don't ask for your soul. Potatoes don't care where you are or even where they are. Tomatoes cuddle up to anyone who'll give them mulch and sunshine. But giants like Max need you every second. You can forget about a whiz-bang social life.

My father, who looked like Abraham Lincoln and played him in the Abraham Lincoln community play every February, felt I didn't have dates because I spent too much time with vegetables. Dad had a theory on everything—God, world hunger, fast food, why I grew giant pumpkins.

"Don't you see, Ellie," he said, "they're big and round and full—"

I sucked in my stomach. "What's your point, Dad?"

He coughed and went into one of his speeches on how pumpkins symbolize my desire for life's fullness and reaching my full potential. "You should be nurturing yourself, Ellie, instead of this . . . vegetable. Spending night and day with a squash is not healthy . . . or fulfilling."

"It's fulfilling to me."

"I know it seems that way now, honey," he continued, bending his 6'6" frame over me.

"And it's fulfilling to Max. Look at him, Dad."

My father scowled at Max and stroked his beard. It's hard to cross Abraham Lincoln. Un-American.

"It is simply not appropriate to have a relationship with a pumpkin, Ellie. Shall we get you a pet of some kind . . . perhaps a dog, a gerbil—"

"I don't want a pet."

I wanted to say that I could use some paternal understanding once in a while. I swatted a fly instead. I wanted to say that he wasn't exactly burning up the dating field either and that maybe social problems ran in the family.

Old Abe gave up for the moment and stood stooped in the field. "I'm afraid your grandmother got you into this," he mumbled, walking away.

Actually, *Cinderella* got me into this. My grandmother, who I call Nana, had the money. I was five when she took me to see the movie, and I was impressed with the pumpkin's starring role. It was the pumpkin the fairy godmother changed first. Everybody thinks the ballgown came first. Wrong. Cinderella

7

drags the pumpkin over, the fairy godmother says, "Salago doola, menchika boola—bibbidi, bobbidi, boo!" Bang, you have your basic magic coach. She couldn't have done that with a zucchini. It would have looked like a bus. Cinderella needed a royal carriage, not exact change and a seat with gum all over it.

Now, over the years Dad has tried to point out the strength of other vegetables in literature. *Jack and the Beanstalk*, for example, but as I argued, the beanstalk got Jack in nothing but trouble. *The Princess and the Pea* is an insomniac's nightmare. I don't think the throne was worth it. Peter Rabbit nearly croaked in the cabbage patch, stumbled home with nausea, heartburn, plus diarrhea, *and* got grounded.

But a pumpkin—now, there was a vegetable with promise.

So it was a love from the very beginning. They were round, I was round. As Nana said, "There's growing and then there's *growing*." You throw some carrot seeds into the ground, when it's harvest time you yank them up, and no big deal. But when you grow pumpkins, people notice. Up they come, big, tough, and sturdy. You get respect.

I had read an article in *Seventeen* about getting along better with your parents, when this whole issue of respect came up. I talked to Richard about how my father didn't respect me. How could we have a relationship without it?

"You could have a bad relationship," Richard suggested, swinging an imaginary bat, which he always did to keep his muscles supple. He was fifteen and a half, but concerned they could go anytime. Athletes are like that.

"I already have a bad relationship with my father," I said. "I want to have a good relationship with him."

"I don't think that's possible."

"Why not?"

"Actually," Richard said, swinging to connect with a tricky curve ball, "it is possible. But you'd have to change everything about yourself."

I looked at my pudgy knees and hands, stained from kneeling and digging in the dirt. I thought of my thin, spotless father in his cottons and tweeds who brushed off a chair before he sat on it whether it needed it or not.

"So what's the answer?" I said.

Richard put down the bat and wiped off his hands. "I think, Ellie, that people respect people that are either like them or people they want to be like."

"So?"

"I think it's a lost cause with your father. Give it up. Be your own person."

"There's got to be something I—"

"Do you have anything in common?" Richard asked.

I thought hard. "Ice cream," I said.

"Then I'd eat a lot of ice cream together and not talk much."

"I'm on a diet."

"You could learn Japanese," he offered, swinging again.

Dad and I sat on the back porch eating coconut ice cream, his favorite. I'd made it by hand with heavy cream, sugar, and lots of Baker's Angel Flake. Dad's face was somewhere in heaven, and my calorie count was enough to sustain a starving Third World nation.

I had wiped Max down with Windex before we went outside so he would sparkle in the moonlight, and placed Dad's favorite chair at just the right angle to catch the gleam.

"Well," I said, "this is nice." My father nodded and kept on eating. "I want you to know, Dad, that I'm starting my diet tomorrow."

"Ellie," he said, dishing out another bowl, "I wish you great luck. If there's anything I can do, I'd like to help. I've had my own battle with weight, of course."

I could hardly remember when he was fat. He was thin now from all that jogging. Two years ago he'd run a marathon at age forty-two and finished in front of a thirty-four-year-old IBM salesman with braces on his teeth.

A wind blew Max's leaves and lifted the summer smells of purple phlox and wild roses. The wild rose was Iowa's state flower, and Rock River yards were full of them, since we had more heart than any town in the state. The stars shone down like sparklers from heaven. Looking south, I could see Lyra (the Lyre), a small constellation that lights the summer sky. A pale blue star glowed at the northern tip.

I pointed: "Vega's out, Dad."

He looked up and smiled. "The fifth-brightest star seen from earth, Ellie." Stars always perked Dad up. He knew all about them and taught me when I was small. We hadn't done much star gazing lately, though, because all of Dad's motivating made him look inside instead of up. I missed it, too. I watched him from the corner of my eye and figured he'd be up half the night again, battling his sleeping dragons. Nana said the hardest part about being a widower is the empty bed at night.

From our back porch I could see frame houses with rows of big yards swallowed up by the moonlight. People here pretty much knew who they were and let their yards say it. This all went out the window when folks became parents of teenagers, since parents of teenagers aren't clear what planet they're on. Hedges go bushy, lawns get grouchy. This didn't happen at my house because I was in charge of the yard. I thought Dad should appreciate that. Being a turncoat grower, he didn't.

We were only a mile from Rock River's real farm country, where the sunsets went on for miles and where, Nana said, the houses never messed with nature. That's where Nana lived and where Dad grew up, but he could never appreciate the greatness of being surrounded by growers. He couldn't understand why anyone would choose a profession that's dependent on something so undependable—the weather.

Dad saw a tornado level a farmer's wheat field when he was twelve years old, and he never got over the injustice. Nana said Dad just jumped from the womb hating farming, and it was a big mystery to her and Grandpa where those renegade genes came from. I figured farming genes can't root in an unresponsive soul. I think what bugs Dad most about me is that I love something he's always resented.

The once mighty Rock River flowed near Nana's property, three feet wide and shrinking. The shrinking had begun five years ago because of increased irrigation over the years. It caused quite a stir when a nasty man from a road atlas company in Iowa City said that Rock River no longer qualified for "true river status" and would be marked on his maps as a "stream." Mannie Plummer, a local grower, said it was typical of Iowa City foreigners. She led an emotional march around Town Hall and got a petition signed with 396 names of people who knew the Rock River when it was something to see. "It's just getting old," Mannie said in her speech in Founders' Square, "like a lot of us." The townspeople nodded, and the man at the atlas company called it a stream anyway, which is why you can't find a decent road atlas in Rock River, Iowa, today.

Our house had been Dad's compromise. He wanted one far enough away from tractors and farmers without moving out of town, and close enough to people who wore suits to work and ate Chinese food. The house we lived in with Mother was too big for the two of us, and Dad couldn't handle the memories. He had a soft spot, though, and found us a new house that let me be a grower within the extreme confines of a half acre.

I was nine when we moved from the old Colonial on Farmer's Road. Dad never goes by it, but I do. I can walk past it now (it's taken some time) without the ache of Mother's death crashing in like waves. Nana taught me that avoiding hard things just makes them harder. Time and love are mighty healers.

Our house is mustard yellow with green shutters. Dad and I painted it together last year, and everyone said it looked fine. I wanted to paint it a gentle pumpkin color, but Dad said, nice try, *absolutely* no. We settled for mustard, a color with warm, positive associations unless you happened to be a ketchup or mayonnaise person.

The backyard is filled with good, rich soil; the sunshine hits bright in the morning, which a pumpkin really appreciates. I had taken most of the space for Max, who was glistening in the moonlight.

Dad was still eating. I should have let the moment be, but I couldn't help myself.

"Doesn't Max look great, Dad?"

I knew this was against the rules. Richard said eat ice cream together, not talk, but I couldn't help it. Dad harrumphed, sitting with his elbow on each armrest like the Lincoln Memorial. A squawking crow flew on top of Max. I bolted up clapping my hands and ran down the path shooing it away as Dad watched silently. I felt a cold chill go through me like an October wind. Strange, since it was only August. Then the miles between Dad and me seemed to race farther apart. I covered Max with an old blanket, patted his stem, and walked back up the porch to eat ice cream with my father.

Chapter Two

Some jerk at the Board of Education decided that school should start before Labor Day this year—just in case there were a lot of snow days—so the seniors could graduate the third week of June, before the mosquitoes hit the creek behind the athletic field. Last year had been a nightmare on graduation night, June 30, as the mosquitoes, drawn by the aroma of Jade East, lilac perfume, and Southern Comfort, descended on ninety-seven seniors without bias or mercy. I was a junior, so it didn't matter to me if the seniors graduated in mid-July wrapped in gauze and the valedictorian got eaten alive by vampire moths. I thought it was stupid and unfair to sit perfectly healthy students in a stifling classroom the last week in August, and I told Richard so.

"You can't postpone the inevitable," he said. "Before Labor Day, after Labor Day, it really doesn't matter."

Richard could say that because he didn't have a

world-class pumpkin to develop. All he had to do was get his batting average up to .350. Max was bursting forth in great, glorious spurts. To leave him now was unthinkable. Who would spray the insects, yank the weeds, shriek at the hungry birds and rabbits, monitor weather conditions, and fend off blight? Do you put a racehorse out to pasture before the Kentucky Derby? While I was imprisoned in chemistry lab, Cyril Pool would be boostering his pumpkin to the thrill of victory.

I discussed this with JoAnn Clark, my absolute best friend, and Grace McKenna, my absolute close second. We decided that Dad had to be reasonable about the important things in life. School didn't work for me right now.

"I'd like to drop out of school until the Weigh-In," I told my father. "I'll continue to study . . . maybe we could get a tutor—"

"Enough!" Dad cried, storming from the garden. He was always irrational when it came to my needs.

"You leave me no choice!" I shouted after him. "I will get up before dawn to tend him. I will walk through school with buckling knees, weary, bleary-eyed—"

Dad turned, and in the shadows he loomed like a mammoth scarecrow. "You will," he boomed, "get eight hours of sleep each night, young lady! Is that clear?"

Crystal.

I lay in bed and watched the clock: 11:19 P.M. He could make me be in bed, but he couldn't make me sleep. Max slumped forlorn outside my window. Noble Max, whose ancestors sustained the Pilgrims through their first winter in America.

That first winter must have been a bust, and you can bet the pumpkins weren't appreciated right off.

Vegetables never are. The Pilgrim children were probably crabbing by December ("Oh, no, pumpkin *again!*"), never realizing a pumpkin had all those disease-fighting nutrients and was a key dietary staple since it was too big to be lugged off the settlement by wild, rabid bears. It just goes to show you that even ancient people couldn't appreciate something right under their noses, which is probably why the Pilgrims became extinct. There's a lesson here for all of us, especially my father.

I opened my window and fixed my eyes on Max. He needed me, and I was a prisoner. There is something about a grower's presence that calls a vegetable to greatness. I waved at him. I would not sleep! Cyril's squash was probably basking in love and adulation and pushing out beyond good taste.

But the air at Cyril's place was polluted with deceit—bad oxygen could work to my advantage. I pictured his pumpkin withering in the patch, lying in defeat; a mere gourd. While this did not show a high sportsmanlike attitude on my part, it felt pretty good. I slept like a baby.

I was up at five-thirty and hurried out to Max. I watered him, wiped him, and sat with him before Dad's "ahem" echoed from the porch. I ate seven bite-size Shredded Wheats with half a banana and six ounces of skim milk, which hardly seemed worth the trouble, but I was going for the gaunt look, and severe measures were required. Dad had coffee.

Richard and I walked to school the long way down Bud DeWitt Memorial Drive, because I wanted to go by Cyril's place to see if anything was new, if you get my meaning. We rounded the turn by the Bud DeWitt Memorial White Hen, where I could hear the freshly

iced doughnuts calling to me from their plastic case. I
do not want a French chocolate glazed, I said to myself.
I am going to be thin and gorgeous. Money burned in
my pocket, but I marched on.

It was at this very White Hen that realtor Bud
DeWitt, who personally sold, rented, and rebuilt two
thirds of Rock River, stopped every morning at 8:00
A.M. to pick up three dozen bismarcks to soften up his
prospects. He died of unknown causes while closing a
deal last fall. When the ambulance came he'd been long
dead with a smile on his face and a bismarck in his fist.

Cyril was the only grower in town who had named
his farm and had a slogan. It was a stupid one at that. It
hung from two whitewashed posts and swung in the
breeze. His aunt had painted it in calligraphy and put
butterflies and smiling faces around the letters. Cyril, I
was sure, would never marry, which was just as well for
future generations, because no one should have to live
with a man with a sign that read: POOL'S PUMPKIN
PATCH, HOME OF THE WHOPPER. Every time I
saw it I wanted to puke. Pumpkins were not cute, they
were majestic, and this was not the sign of a champion.
The man should be disqualified from all growing com-
petitions for bad taste alone.

A truck was parked in the field, and Cyril was
pouring liquids into a can and shaking it. The can was
unmarked, of course. Growers guard their secret
booster solutions like McDonald's protects their special
sauce recipe. Cyril saw me, covered his can, and smiled
just enough to let all his bad teeth show.

"Well, Missy," he said, "come to check out the competition?"

I hated it when he called me "Missy." Cyril called
every woman under seventy he met "Missy" because he

17

was bad at names. Actually, Cyril was bad at life in general.

"Just passing through," I lied, shoving Richard ahead of me.

"Brought your spy with you, I see," Cyril said, indicating Richard, who glared back. "Well, feast your eyes on it, Missy, and weep."

A man jumped in the truck and drove it a few yards away, revealing the pumpkin, the sight of which made me stop breathing. It was enormous, bigger and fuller than Max, with orange skin so bright it looked like it had been painted on. Knowing Cyril, it probably had been. It had a sign next to it that read BIG DADDY.

"Whatcha think?" Cyril leered, wiping his hands on his filthy overalls.

Richard hit me on the back to start me breathing again. I collected myself nice and cool. "You call that a pumpkin?" I said, mocking. Well, you should have seen Cyril's face. It nearly caved in, and Richard swallowed a laugh so hard he was coughing and bent over just trying to control himself.

Cyril rose to full 5′4″ height and smacked down his oily hair, his eyes on fire. "I call that a *champeen* pumpkin, Missy," he spat. "Better'n anything you've ever seen."

"Make some child a real nice jack-o'-lantern, Cyril," I said. "Have a nice day."

I grabbed Richard, who had dropped his lunch all over the road from the laughing, and we ran off like little kids who had just rung some old codger's doorbell for the fifteenth time.

This wasn't my normal approach with people, but Cyril had it coming, especially since he'd been sticking it to me ever since last year's Harvest Fair, when he beat me by 91.3 pounds. When he said, loud enough for the world to hear, that maybe I wasn't ready to enter the adult growing competition and couldn't they find him a more formidable opponent. Cyril didn't say "formidable" because he didn't use words more than six letters long. I was angry, let me tell you, but managed to act like a champion even though I'd lost.

I learned this from Nana, who said that the way to continue the great Morgan family tradition of growing was to be a winner even when you came in last and wanted to curl up and die. It was up to me to carry the torch, since Dad had walked away from farming when he was twelve, never looking back, and his brother Bill had gone into commercial insurance in Sandusky after flunking out of Buckman's College of Chiropractics and getting Sue Ann Gleason pregnant.

Nana and I were cut from the same cloth. When my mother died, Nana bundled me up in her arms and made me her own. It was Nana who taught me how to grow pumpkins and stand up for what you believe in. "Got the easy part," Nana always said, "growing you in that good soil your mama already worked."

Dad stomped down his memories, but Nana never let me forget. On my thirteenth birthday Nana gave me what's become my most special possession: the journal Mother wrote during the first four months of my life. The inside flap opens to a rose petal drawing, and underneath my mother wrote something that always makes me cry: "To my precious daughter, who will make the world a better place." I hoped I would. Max and I are sure working on it.

On those pages are all her thoughts about motherhood and how she loved it. She recorded when I moved my head and made important noises. She said I was an extremely intelligent baby who battled disease like a champion. She wrote about the high fever I had when I was three months old, how she and Dad took turns holding me in a cool shower to bring it down. There were photographs of Dad in an antler hat by the Christmas tree, of Mother putting a little crown of flowers on my bald head. The last page is dated April 3: "Going back to work tomorrow," it reads. "Bringing Ellie with me."

She did, too. Brought me every day to Redmont's Florist Shop, where I was very well behaved and communed with nature. Mother said I had a grower's heart. Nana said it takes one to know one.

I've read the journal on each birthday since, and I don't think it was possible to have been more loved. Mother was always laughing; that's my best memory of her. Everyone remembered her laugh. She could turn it on Dad and make him not as serious. She'd surprise us with candlelight dinners, and the house seemed to glow in the light of her love. Nana said Mother sometimes hid behind the laughing, afraid of the serious person underneath. Nana wasn't being critical when she said it, I just know what she meant. I don't laugh and joke near as much as Mother did, but I hide sometimes, too. I still have an ache when I think about her; Nana said that's real natural.

I was in gym class when Mother died. We were running laps around the field when Miss Carroll, the school nurse, took me out of class. She said my aunt and grandmother needed to see me, but her face said it was more than that. I shoved down fear as we walked down the old hall that had seemed friendly just minutes before. Aunt Peg and Nana were waiting for me in the principal's office, their faces caved in under a deep sadness. Miss Carroll left quietly, and Nana told me Mother had got hit by a car crossing the street in front of Redmont's Florist Shop. I asked when I could see her, and Aunt Peg started crying bad. I was crying, too, and Nana picked me up with her full strength and said that wasn't going to happen.

I remember the tears after that and the absolute deadness. We rode to Nana's in Aunt Peg's new Buick. I didn't believe Mother could be gone, but I was crying like I did. People were already gathering to share our loss. It was really the loss of the whole town, that's what Mannie Plummer said. Dad was crumpled and broken. He lifted me up to his giant chest and we cried for days and days.

The funeral came and went like a blur. Everyone said how sorry they were. Everyone asked if I wanted something to eat. The minister said Mother was "one of the finest lights God had ever made." Richard gave me his very best baseball. Nana saw I'd had enough and drove me to a hidden field outside of town that was filled with wildflowers. We put together the biggest bouquet you'd ever seen. Nana said she'd always be there for me, no matter what. She has been, too.

Richard refused to go back to school until I did. When we finally went back, a few kids avoided me, like death was something you could catch. My real friends were there, though, and they stuck to my side, helping me without knowing it to push toward normal. Once I wrote about living without my mother. I said life seemed gray and small—like watching black-and-white TV when you're used to big-screen color. Dad put my story in a box in his closet where he keeps his special things.

Memories were part of me, but Nana taught me

not to live in them. We're forever a part of the people who love us, she said. That kind of love is always alive.

Nana is God's gift to me. She is unmovable on being your own person and had a lot of practice standing tall on that one, since Grandpa nearly lost the farm four times because he was too stubborn to admit his mistakes. So she had to step in and remind him who he was and who he wasn't.

"You're a farmer, Willard," she'd say, "not an accountant. If God meant you to be good at numbers, you'd be good at numbers, but for now we've got that crop to bring in, and if you say we don't have the money to do it, then we're just going to have to sell the piano, that's all."

Nana sold the piano four times and always bought it back when times were good. Grandpa never got an accountant till the day he died. He got a calculator, though, but never believed it could really add.

Pumpkin growing wasn't something that Nana knew much about, but she learned it real quick when I showed an interest. Like Mother, Nana could make anything grow, and she passed that on to me. Every flower that could root in Iowa soil was in her front yard. Come midspring people started driving by Nana's house just to get a look at that garden. She had tulips, daffodils, and big, stocky snapdragons; a huge bed of bloodroots, marsh marigolds, roses, petunias, and lilies of the valley growing three deep along her stone path just waiting for elves to give them a shake. One year a whole busload of Japanese students on their way to Des Moines stopped and were squatting on the lawn, taking pictures. Nana made them old-fashioned limeade and served it on the porch in plastic cups.

My father could make anything die just from passing by it. He didn't have a sensitive grower's soul, and the plants *knew*. I've seen petunias give up when they saw Dad coming. So growing pumpkins was a good bet for me living with a man like that. I wouldn't think of laying in chervil or kale or sugar snap peas, because Dad's vibes would dry them right up. I had wildflowers that a crazed hog couldn't kill in big clumps around the house and a bumper crop of New Jersey tomatoes. When Dad watered the lawn I just let natural selection take over. Some tomatoes croaked, and some got tough. The true test of any vegetable is how it fares in the face of adversity.

I wondered how Cyril's pumpkin got so orange living as it did in that environment. I began to think that Dad's vibrations were worse than I'd figured. Clearly, Max was at risk. It was going to take a lot of ice cream to keep Dad mellow.

Richard said to talk to Mr. Greenpeace, Rock River High's most sensitive teacher, who contemplated on weekends and taught beginning philosophy and track. He had an album of gentle sound effects like waterfalls and ocean waves that could reprogram Dad's vibes. Mr. Greenpeace didn't give a rip about protocol, so everyone took his classes, even track, and learned to become "one with the road." He got tenure before he became sensitive, he often said, and everyone was glad about that, except the other teachers, the principal, and the members of the School Board.

He let me borrow the album because he said he'd never seen anyone become as "one with the road" as me. Richard became one with his bat, glove, and ball and didn't care much about what was below. Being a grower, I understood the ground and its virtues. I carried the album home, dimmed the lights, threw coconut, sugar, vanilla, and heavy cream into the ice cream maker, shoved a chicken with rosemary and lemon in the oven, and waited for my father.

He was boiling when he came home, and I could feel Max shudder in response. I had read another article in *Seventeen* about parental tension and was prepared for any outburst. I found the "Waterfall/Soft" portion on the record, pointed the speakers in Dad's direction, and let 'er rip.

"Glad to see you, Dad," I cooed. "Welcome home." The article said not to ask too many questions or make any demands upon a parent's entrance. Really throw him.

"Well," he grumbled, surprised, "you're the first person today who's been glad to see me."

"Oh?" I said. This is the open invitation to talk, but it is in the parent's court. Open, caring, not pushy.

He slumped in his chair away from the speakers, which I now repositioned with my foot. "It was like a bad dream," he groused. "Frederika double-scheduled me for the second time this *month*. I had to cancel with Iowa Federal, and they were furious, of course."

"Of course . . ." I agreed, building camaraderie.

"You would think that after all these years, she would have learned!" He rose and walked to the window, glaring out at nothing, but Max was in his view and growing paler. Bad, bad vibes. I steered him back to his chair as "Waterfall/Soft" gave way to "Waves II."

"I have this sudden impulse," he muttered, "to get near water, Ellie . . . I—"

"Just relax, Dad," I cooed, arranging him in his plaid BarcaLounger, putty in my hands.

"I am so terribly relaxed, Ellie," he whispered. "I just can't tell you."

Now, I could have gotten a raise in allowance from him just then, a car, my own MasterCard, but I had Max to consider. Perhaps a small cash settlement, I thought . . . but no! Max was being infested with conflict and hostility. I would not sell out.

"You asked him for *nothing*?" Richard shrieked the next day, incredulous. "Not even five bucks?"

"I felt that would have been unethical," I explained.

"You trick your father into relaxing and you're talking about ethics?"

"I didn't trick him, Richard. I reprogrammed his environment."

"But he could have popped for something!" Richard railed. "I mean, it sounds like you really had him, Ellie. Movie tickets . . . jeez, I don't know. . . ." He examined his old fielder's mit, scowling. "A new glove . . ."

"I don't play baseball, Richard."

"Then it wouldn't have been an unethical request, you know?"

As a partial baseball star, Richard approached life differently than us mere mortals. He was always looking for ways to make the play. Richard felt if three men were in the outfield the smartest one would make the play even if it meant running into another's territory and knocking him down. This did not bring Richard, the center fielder, favor with Howie Bucks or Farley Raker, the left and right fielders, but the fans loved it, and Mr. Soboleski, the coach, smacked Richard hard on the back like coaches do and shouted, "Way to go, Awesome Ace!" Richard felt every team needed a star and it might as well be him.

We stopped at Nana's after school because I was out of compost mixture for Max and I wanted to talk to her about Cyril's pumpkin. Nana was a multiple blue-ribbon winner at various fairs and knew the pressure of competition.

I couldn't spend much time because I had a five-hundred-word essay due tomorrow for Miss Moritz's world history class on "Churchill's Dilemma." This was Miss Moritz's first year of teaching and she was on a mission from God to fill our minds with enthusiasm for world events. Churchill faced many dilemmas, she cried passionately. Who could name some? We came up with Hitler, who was enough dilemma for anyone. Burma, Malaya. Miss Moritz scrunched up her face and said *that* was the point of the exercise. The list went on and on. Pick the dilemma *we* found most intriguing. I decided to go for the long shot and outlined a sensitive discussion of Churchill's weight problem that I felt deserved five hundred words and my time.

This was risky, since Miss Moritz was quite thin and possibly unable to identify with the dilemma of obesity as it applied to World War II. But weight was my forte, and thinking about Hitler all night would have soaked the house in bad vibes. I had enough problems.

Nana made limeade and put out her soft fudge cookies. The three of us sat outside stuffing ourselves and swatting bugs. From Nana's back porch you could look out past a large vegetable garden to the fields and a painted fence that seemed to end at the sky. Being a farmer, she kept one eye on the land where her heart was, even if she was talking to you real serious. Nana's place always gave me hope because I knew I was on good soil that hadn't failed. Dad started sneezing whenever he got close to the barn.

I could talk to Nana about anything, and I did now, fears rushing off my tongue about Cyril's pumpkin, which was already as big as Cleveland and my rotten luck. Richard ate cookies and squished a bee in his glove as Nana rocked back and forth, full of her special wisdom.

"One of the saddest things in life," Nana began, "is to take something that gives you joy and let it get ruined." She poured more limeade and looked at me like she had a microscope.

"I'm not doing that, Nana. It's Cyril Pool. He's—"

Nana held up her hand and looked at me hard. "Ellie," she said, "as long as you're watching Cyril you're going to miss the point—"

"But—"

"The *point*," she continued, pointing to her heart, "starts here."

"I know that, Nana."

"Well, then you've got to act like it, that's all."

This was Nana's favorite speech, and she had cut it down considerably since I was a child. I knew it from memory. It was about how true winning starts and ends in our heart. Blue ribbons come next—maybe, maybe not. I figured Cyril was a definite challenge to this rule, since his heart was full of rot and he had all those first-place sashes.

"But what about Cyril, Nana? He's going to win again and—"

"Maybe," said Nana, watching the sky. "Maybe

27

not." She leaned back in her old wicker rocker and brushed a ladybug off her housedress. I knew what she was thinking, and she was right as usual. She handed me two bags of compost mixture.

Richard had finished the fudge cookies and was brushing the crumbs off his glove. "Guess we'd better go," I said, rising. "I've got a squash to tend."

"I guess you'd better," Nana echoed, and hugged me so hard that her whole body shook. Whatever Nana did she did with her whole self.

Richard went home to eat with his mother. He figured she needed company every so often, and I was fixing diet salad, which he said could really mess up his game. Dad was the keynote speaker at Sommerset Electric's annual meeting and wouldn't be home till late. Motivating electrical people, Dad groaned, always took time.

I dug around Max and patted Nana's compost evenly around the roots. Pumpkins need well-drained, fertile soil, and I wasn't taking any chances. Big vine types like Max were heavy feeders and drank lots of water. I poured the water slowly around him, waiting as it soaked down to the feeding roots two to three feet underground. That's the secret to watering, and it separates the great growers from the hacks. Most people just dump the water on, since they've got better things to do than hang around and wait. My feeling is if you've got better things to do, you shouldn't be growing pumpkins. It takes patience, that's all. Grow cactuses if you don't care, buy plastic plants and silk flowers. I watered carefully away from the foliage. Wet leaves can cause disease, and that's all I needed. Max had been bug-free all summer, and I wasn't about to get sloppy now.

I poured my secret booster solution into a steel dish and adjusted the wick I'd positioned in a slit in Max's vine. There was still enough light to begin my second draft of "Churchill's Dilemma," which I aptly subtitled, "The Weight of World War II." Max drank the solution happily. My stomach groaned from starvation. I wrote and rewrote, creating a Churchill few had considered. "Perhaps," I penned in my final summation, "the greatness of Winston Churchill lay not only in his ability to bear the weight of much of World War II, but in his ability to bear his own considerable weight as well."

Dad's voice broke my creative cocoon. "Ellie!" he yelled. "Do you know what time it is?"

I didn't, but guessed he would tell me.

"It's ten o'clock, young woman, and you're out here sitting with . . . vegetation." He said "vegetation" like what he really meant was "lepers."

And Winston Churchill, Dad. A highly motivated individual and world leader who only thought great thoughts and reached his full potential. My father stood at the screen door and held it open. There was no defying him. I sighed, gathered my work, and lumbered inside.

"I *was* doing my homework," I said.

"With a vegetable in the dirt—"

"With an award-winning squash in the moonlight."

Just once, could he try to see what I see? But I knew the answer: I saw Max; Dad saw pumpkin pie.

Dad let out a slow, sad sigh. I was determined to make contact and punched his arm playfully. "Did ya motivate 'em tonight, Dad? All those boring electrical people?"

Old Abe turned and managed a grin. I loved it when he smiled, because it healed his whole face. "Expect big things from Sommerset Electric in the months to come, Ellie."

I nodded. "Like better electricity?"

"Unquestionably," said Dad. "They bought sixty-seven success tapes and thirty-one books."

"Ah," I said. "And did they feed you at this thing?"

"Grilled ox. Well done."

I groaned, sliced a hunk of my famous whole wheat Irish soda bread, and slathered it with plum preserves. He dug in as Max gleamed in the moonlight. I lit a candle on the kitchen table for peace, and wondered if motivational therapy worked on squashes.

Chapter
Three

I **got a C minus** on my "Churchill's Dilemma" essay, which I thought was stingy, since it brought my grade average down, but it was typical of a sneaky, skinny person like Miss Moritz. She said: "Your writing is imaginative, Ellie. If you had picked a less unorthodox approach . . ." I felt if she'd picked an approach that students could relate to or been hired by another school none of this would have happened. Richard said new teachers couldn't help themselves, having been filled with all that poop in college. It was up to each student to wait them out until their enthusiasm died.

It was outside Miss Moritz's class that I first saw Wes, the new boy, and I felt like I'd been bonged in the head with a Crenshaw melon. He was tall, a plus since I was five-seven, not gorgeous, you understand, but okay-looking and not too thin. He had dark glasses and wavy black hair and a great laugh that seemed to start in his stomach and work its way up.

I knew a few things about him, too. He was a

grower. Not just *a* grower, the president of the Agricultural Club at Gaithersville High before his father got promoted to national sales manager of Wycliffe Feed and Grain and transferred up here to the big city. And if you were a grower and knew the ropes like me, you knew that Gaithersville had a heavy Ag Club.

Wes grew sweet corn—a perfectly reasonable vegetable—not showy, but nice. Iowa, after all, was called "the land where the tall corn grows," which got people's hearts thumping if they were into corn and didn't do much for anybody else. He'd grown a lot of it in Gaithersville and was going to plant some here in early spring. He was going to be a farmer and attend Texas A&M which was next to heaven. I knew all this because Grace McKenna was his cousin, and Grace never left anything out. Where Wes was concerned, I wanted to know *everything*.

First off, it's important you know I am not boy-crazy. I don't flirt and bat my eyes like Sharrell Upton and the rest of the squealing cheerleaders. Most of the boys I know, except Richard, who doesn't count, don't care about growing, and that's where we part company. I'm not going to spend my time with a brain-dead male who doesn't know the difference between a Big Max and a begonia.

Grace told me that Wes was brokenhearted about moving and having a hard time adjusting to Rock River's fast Des Moines area pace. He had a girlfriend back in Gaithersville (bad news) who he still saw on weekends (worse news), but Grace didn't think it was exactly love. Anyway, it had been raining like a monster for the past five days, and getting to Gaithersville in this weather wasn't worth it no matter who you had waiting down there. I had lost six of the seven pounds I gained from all that worry and butterscotch swirl ice cream, and had twenty-one more to go. Grace said Wes and I were perfect for each other. I was glad to hear that because this diet was getting to me.

Max, being a pumpkin, was not crazy about the rain, and if it didn't stop soon I was going to have to take drastic action. Cyril had already covered his Atlantic Giant with reemay cloth, a light, gauzy blanket that kept bugs and frost off pumpkins. I always felt waiting longer than Cyril was wise, since the man was technically a sludge and didn't know the first thing about making an informed decision.

How a pumpkin ever grew on its own is beyond me, because keeping one going is an everyday fight. Any soft place on the skin was the kiss of death in this weather. Absolute doom. I've seen giants that could have gone all the way just cave in, full of rot inside because their growers couldn't read the weather and didn't know when to fight back. I tapped Max's skin and inspected his leaves and stem carefully for any signs of rot, beaming healthy, fat thoughts through his vine. He was clean and solid and I planned to keep him that way. He knew it, too.

Richard heard Cyril had another woodchuck problem in his patch. Good news for me, especially if the woodchucks were eating Big Daddy. He was shooting them and cussing them at night, lighting flare guns, and making terrible threats. It was just like Cyril to climb into a tank to fight against woodchucks instead of just putting up a fence. If it wasn't loud and in bad taste, Cyril wouldn't try it. Nana said Cyril was blessed with good soil to make up for everything else God didn't give him. Everybody wanted to beat Cyril real bad, but nobody wanted to as much as me.

Growers are driven by their insides and aren't afraid of hard work. Mr. Warnock began the fine art of giant pumpkin growing back in 1900. The man had great vision and great vines. His 403-pounder from the 1904 St. Louis World's Fair wasn't beat until 1976. That's the kind of competitor you want to go up against. He makes the whole process a clean challenge. It bugged me that Cyril turned competition into a hateful thing. Nana said it was because he had so much nastiness inside.

This rain was beginning to worry me, and I had a plastic covering ready to throw over Max if need be. Most growers had a bigger patch of land than me and could grow several giants at once, so losing one wasn't so bad. Dad didn't want a lot of land because he'd sold his soul when he left farming. Raising an only pumpkin took guts because you had no fallback position. I just put all my eggs in one basket and killed myself trying.

I was thankful Dad never managed to leave Rock River. He and Mother were going to live in California after they got married, but Grandpa fell off the barn roof fixing a hole and needed someone around to help. Dad stayed, but Nana said it was tough going: "Biggest mistake your grandpa ever made was insisting your father love farming."

I looked at Max and knew he was feeling the barometric pressure. The rain kept coming, and that sky just sat there looking dark and mean. Another day of showers could make the difference between a blue ribbon and pie filling.

I woke up at 2:00 A.M. The rain was pounding off the roof. I pulled on my jeans, grabbed my slicker and plastic sheet, and ran outside to dress Max. He was soaked through, puddles surrounded him, the ground too wet to absorb all the water. I dug three runoff channels, slapped on the plastic, and lay over him like a hen covering her brood. The lightning cracked, the ground rumbled from the thunder. I figured I must be near crazy to love a vegetable this much.

The rain was cold and soaked clear to my bones. A chill flew over me that a grower rarely feels until October. I knew if Dad saw me hanging over Max he'd ground me for life, but Max needed support and warmth, and nobody who grew giant pumpkins ever did it for their health. The rain poured down in sloppy buckets. Lightning lashed the sky, coming in so close I could feel the heat. If this didn't let up soon I was going to fry or start building an ark.

At dawn the storm broke. I was half dead, but managed to push past it. I cut pieces of hose to suck out the floods of water around Max, running it back down the small hill into the rock garden Nana and I had planted. Nana would understand. You can always find more rocks. Max was drier now and warm under the plastic. I slipped inside for dry clothes, knowing I would have to lie about why I had to stay home from school.

"It's my throat, Dad," I said, freshly dressed, dried, and looking miserable. "I feel awful." Dad felt my clammy forehead and bought in. I am an honest person who doesn't use sickness as an excuse unless it is absolutely necessary. Missing school meant I couldn't watch Wes, but today school and honesty were out of the question.

Dad took forever to leave that morning. I lay in bed waiting, groaning appropriately, sipping cranberry juice. The sun was blasting out, and Max was sucking it up. You could be the greatest pumpkin grower in the world, which I almost was, but without the sun, you might as well be farming radishes. Dad left finally. I ran to the field and began emergency care.

I dried Max off with clean cloths, inspecting him for any sign of beetles or fungus, ran four electrical cord extensions into the house, fired up my hair dryer, and dried his leaves good right there in the field. Between the hot air and sun Max was feeling his old self and stretching to grow. I dug the wet surface dirt away and patted down two bags of my special mixture of soil, peat moss, and pearlite. The breakfast of champions. He was drying fine now. I covered him with a reemay cloth to keep him a few degrees warmer. The hoses had the flooding under control.

It was eleven o'clock. Wes was just getting out of band and cleaning his clarinet. This was a good place to watch him because he took great care cleaning that instrument. I watched Wes whenever I could, which took some doing, since we had no classes together and our lockers were on different floors. Grace wanted to introduce us right away, but I wanted to lose a few more pounds. I'd be wearing my khaki pants, which don't fit when I'm above 140 pounds, my floppy orange silk blouse, and my mother's gold dangly earrings, which make me look deeply sophisticated. I ate hardly anything because I was going to get into those khaki pants if it killed me. It probably would.

Grace had sent out invitations to her annual beginning-of-school bash. The only year she didn't have it was when she got mono from kissing Jimmy Schroeder, but otherwise it was during the fourth week of school, and *everyone* came. Grace didn't think much about the party, it was really for her mother. Grace was the youngest of four children by eight years, and Mrs. McKenna was hanging on for dear life.

Mrs. McKenna wanted Grace to attend Drake University in Des Moines to keep an eye on her, but Grace was looking east, far east, to Tokyo or Hong Kong. Grace figured a four-hour flight to Los Angeles followed by twelve hours to Tokyo with all that white rice and no potatoes would finish her mother off good. Mrs. McKenna split a gut when she heard this and refused to pay for any education east of Chicago, a seven-hour car trip if you made two bathroom stops and ate lunch in the car.

It was not good to cross Mrs. McKenna. She was the reigning secretary until death of the Rock River Pumpkin Weigh-In and Harvest Fair—*the* entertainment event of the year, the town's number one moneymaker, and my only hope for achieving greatness. Mrs. McKenna called it "Probably the Greatest Free Show on Earth (at Least in Iowa)" and talked about it in her sleep. She dressed in orange for the whole four days and personally rang the town bell that closed the schools for the long weekend. The woman was connected. No grower worth his salt would so much as belch in her direction.

Grace's party was a lesser affair, but a good excuse for Mrs. McKenna to bake, eavesdrop, and interfere, all of which she did very well. I could do without Grace's party because I did better in small groups, but Dad got worked up when the invitation came. Anything that would get me away from Max for an evening and hopefully propel me to popularity was fine by him.

"Well," he said, beaming. "Well. Won't *this* be nice?"

Being popular was important to Dad, since he had achieved it late in life, having been a nerd when he was younger. I knew popularity wasn't all roses and that Dad was expecting something of me he couldn't achieve in his own youth. Richard said this was typical of parents—wanting Willie Mays to *also* take piano lessons so he'd be popular at parties in case his career went belly up.

Nana said to be patient with Dad because a part of him died when Mother did: "He used all those motivating words to build a hedge around himself" was how Nana described it. "Kept the hurt from oozing out."

So I chewed my lip as Dad kept yakking about Grace's party. Who was going? What was I going to wear? Maybe some nice boy and I would hit it off. I chewed until I drew blood.

"Everyone's going and I don't know what I'm going to wear," I said finally. "Maybe a gorilla suit."

"Ellie," my father droned, "I am not your enemy. I simply mean to suggest that this dress-for-success business works. I have seen it transform dreary lives. We project to others what we really feel about ourselves. If our clothes shout dull, not interested—"

"I do not have a 'dreary' life." Usually.

"I didn't say you did, honey. I simply meant that fragile self-esteem can be corrected and that—"

"I don't have 'fragile self-esteem,'" I insisted, looking at my broken fingernails and mud-caked jeans. I hated it when he sounded like one of his motivational tapes. "*Fragile people* do not grow giant pumpkins, Dad."

"Ellie," he continued, "as your father who loves you and who is also a specialist in success and motivating others, it is my professional opinion that you are standing at the end of the line when you could be out in front leading the big parade."

By "end of the line" he meant agriculture—the Absolute Dead-End Existence, according to Dad. I bet if I'd picked anything outside of farming he'd support me. Reptile Research: "Well," he'd say, "that's certainly a motivated lizard you've got there, Ellie. Keep up the good work." As for "leading the big parade," I'd done that once. I was a sixth-grade Girl Scout and dropped the American flag on Porter McIntyre's grave in the Memorial Day ceremony. It lay on the ground as the high school band played "The Star-Spangled Banner." Two shaky old VFW guys hauled it away to burn it.

"Leading the parade is one of life's great thrills," he continued. "It is not only a great honor, but a responsibility as well."

Now, the articles I've read about getting along with your parents say that when the battle's lost, *do not* start another war. But being a grower, I took special pride in doing things myself and wasn't too keen on turning outside for help. When you can nurture a plant and turn a seed into a giant, you get your strength from the land, something impossible for nongrowers to understand. Which is why Wes fit the boyfriend bill, but I sure wasn't going to tell Dad that.

"I'll think about it," I said.

Dad sighed and gave me his Old Abe stare. He took off his reading glasses, folded them like they were made of diamonds, and put them in his breast pocket. He patted me on the shoulder and walked away, slowly for emphasis.

I checked Max, who looked good despite the pressure. His vine had lifted two feet off the ground. I felt clunky and dumb and misunderstood. I covered his leaves with insecticide and wondered if the spray worked on fathers.

I weighed 144 pounds and was dreaming about chocolate chip cheesecake. Max weighed 430 pounds and was dreaming about victory. I hadn't had any sugar for three weeks and was going through withdrawal—the heavy emotional variety. I watched a Sara Lee pound cake commercial on TV and burst into tears. At midnight I hacked a frozen fudge pie with an ice pick before tossing it in the garbage. I stole Richard's Twinkie from his backpack, and he caught me tearing the wrapper off with my teeth. Richard said this was a sign that my diet should end. He could say that because his khaki slacks always fit. Grace's party was three days off.

I'd found a new hairdo that involved braiding the hair with a ribbon and letting it drape elegantly over one shoulder. I had a thick ribbon that matched my orange blouse and began perfecting the braiding process to one hour and twenty minutes. Richard felt hair was for putting under baseball caps and didn't understand the concept of glamour.

"What's that?" he said, eating a Snickers as I emerged from the bathroom after my first trial run.

"A *braid*," I said, eyeing the candy. Milk chocolate, peanuts, caramel.

"You look different."

"I'm *supposed* to look different."

Richard considered this, eating his Snickers slowly. He did not cope well with change and often slept in the last row of Mrs. Vernon's seventh-period freshman study hall, where he had snoozed all last year, forgetting he was now a sophomore.

"Richard," Mrs. Vernon would say, "how old are

you?" Richard would think before he replied, because age to him was relative, and he'd been awakened from a deep coma. The little freshman girls would start giggling, and Richard would shuffle out to seventh-period sophomore study hall, where the desks weren't nearly as comfortable, feeling that school was tough enough without having your sleep patterns interrupted.

Richard touched my braid, unsure. "Are you going to look like this from now on?" he asked sadly.

"Not every day, no."

"Good," he said.

I retreated to the bathroom for another braiding. I was wearing a T-shirt with a corn stalk that said MAIZE on the front. Wes's girlfriend was safe in Gaithersville, and Grace was finally going to introduce us. I was ready.

I had read up on growing corn—not in Max's presence, certainly, but off-hours. Corn was a noble vegetable—strange how I'd never seen that before. What was more beautiful than a golden field of corn against a summer sunset? A gargantuan pumpkin from my patch covered with first-place victory ribbons and basking in applause and adulation was the only thing I could think of. Without corn, where would America be? Think of all those hogs dying in their slop without a corn husk to munch on. Think of sitting down to a big plate of barbecue with nothing but lima beans on the side for roughage. It made you thankful there were men like Wes who cared about their country. Corn farmers were solid people. Pure, honest, American.

"Like baseball," Richard said, bouncing his ball off a passing barn roof and catching it, running. "You like him, don't you?"

"Who?" I said, horrified my secret was out.

41

"Oh, come on, Ellie!"

I told Richard I didn't want to talk about it, and he said fine, neither did he. As a partial baseball star, he'd been invited to Grace's party even though he was a lowly sophomore and not worthy of the honor. Richard was going in formal attire, which meant without his ball and glove. Dad, unfortunately, was driving us. And Dad had this thing about being on time.

"Promptness or lack of it is the first definition of a person," he announced throughout my childhood. "Lateness is sloppy, Ellie. Often seen in persons with low self-esteem."

Or persons with two feet of hair to braid. It had taken one hour and fifty-five minutes today because I was nervous, but I finally got the braid to look like the one in the picture. Dad marched in to tell me what time it was and that we were going to be late.

"The thing is, Dad," I said, deciding not to get ruffled no matter what, "it's best to get to these things a little late. Let the party get started, you know. Make a big entrance."

He backed off and I was thankful we were only driving Richard who handled Dad by talking baseball. He was back again and looked at me strangely. "You look very pretty tonight," Dad murmured. "Very much like your mother."

That really knocked me out and I wasn't sure what to say except thank you. His eyes got fuzzy and he went outside to start the car. I went into my room, opened my top bureau drawer, and took out the picture of my mother and father on their honeymoon, arm in arm, walking down the beach.

I studied my mother's face but couldn't find the resemblance. She was small and delicate, with laughter flowing out of her. Dad's face was filled with love, much different than now. I think Dad got as close to his roots as he ever would when he married Mother.

I wondered how things would have turned out if she hadn't died. She probably would have helped me with my braid. She used to braid my hair. On Sundays she'd tie my braids with lacy bows that matched my church dresses. I remembered how gentle she was and funny and how well she played the guitar, which everyone told her but she never believed. I remembered how Dad always wanted her to open her own florist shop and get lots of clients. But Mother would just laugh and then do something crazy like shove a bunch of snapdragons down his shirt, and that would be the end of that.

She was good for my father because she softened him. Her name was Claire, but Dad called her "Clairie," a big deal for Dad, who called Pete Ninsenzo, the garbageman, "Mr. Ninsenzo." I could have talked to her about Wes and she would have listened.

And I know she would have understood about Max. She would have been crazy about him for sure. Mother grew roses—damasks, climbers, and brilliant yellow briers—they filled the yard, the smell of them sweetening every room of the house. People who grow roses understand deep things, Nana said, because they know about touching greatness.

Dad was honking in the driveway, so I put the picture back in the drawer underneath my good underwear. I was wearing my standby black pants but suddenly felt lucky. I sucked in my stomach, tried on the khaki slacks, and froze at the sight. They fit! Snug, yes, not perfect, but I could still breathe, sort of. And like Richard said, if you wait for perfect you'll never make the play.

I tossed my head to watch Mother's earrings dance and headed for the stairs, taking them easy to not create tension in the seams. I swept past Max who would have made a perfect carriage, and into Dad's waiting Toyota.

"We're late," Dad announced, pulling away. Some coachman.

"To the palace," I said.

"I beg your pardon?"

"Let's get Richard," I tried again.

Chapter Four

Richard **was developing** his left-hand swing on the front lawn. Richard, a right-hander, figured a switch-hitter was worth a few hundred thousand more in salary with the Chicago Cubs, so he taped his right arm to his side last February to strengthen his grip. This drove his mother crazy because in addition to having a one-armed son, she had a house full of broken dishes that Richard dropped when it was his turn to dry. She hung a sign in the kitchen that read: IF YOU BREAK IT, YOU BOUGHT IT. Richard lost most of his allowance that month to breakage fees, but felt that commercial endorsements would more than make up for it when he hit the pros.

Being Richard, he didn't say anything about how great I looked. He and Dad talked about the influence of the Japanese on baseball and the universe. I was squeezed in the backseat, thin and stunning, my feet straddling a pile of Dad's best-selling success tapes: *You and You Alone.* I could see my perfect makeup job in Dad's rearview mirror. I tightened my lips to make my cheekbones show.

Dad, who normally didn't put the top up on his convertible until the first snow every year, stopped the car, snapped up the roof, and said, "Your mother never liked convertibles." I sat real quiet, like you do in the presence of something delicate. We drove in silence to Grace's.

Dad pulled up the driveway of the McKennas' three-story peach frame house. It had white shutters and gingerbread trim, like a doll cottage come to life. The lawn was freshly mowed, the walk lined with potted yellow mums. The bushes twinkled with Christmas lights in the middle of September.

"Have fun, you two," Dad boomed, patting my hand.

Richard swaggered down the walk, knowing he was going to be accepted because he was a recognized athlete. I followed behind slowly, not wanting to test the strength of my seams. The night was dry and warm—perfect pumpkin conditions.

"What's that stuff on your face?" Richard asked.

I was horrified and said, "Makeup," like it was no big deal.

"What're those clumpy things on your eyes?" he continued.

"I think," I snapped, "they're called *eyelashes.*"

I could hear the party sounds from inside as Richard and I stood by the door. Perhaps a kind family would adopt me so I could have another cousin. Richard said maybe I needed to wash my face to get the gunk off and that I should have done that before we left, all of which made me feel like an ugly troll. We rang the bell, which didn't ding, dong, or buzz. It tinkled. "Just like laughing fairies," Mrs. McKenna always said. The fairies' laughter didn't carry too well, so Richard crashed the door knocker until Mrs. McKenna appeared, plump and happy in her frilliest apron. She said we certainly did look nice, and were we ready for a good time? Richard said he guessed he was as I lunged past her for the bathroom to check for clumping. The door was locked. I waited in the shadows.

Grace's party got Mrs. McKenna rolling for the Rock River Pumpkin Weigh-In and Harvest Fair and its pressures. No one is sure how she became its reigning secretary until death, and no one was going to ask her because Mrs. McKenna *was* the festival. The last day of the fair, when the sixty-cent taffy apples were going for a quarter and Marion Avenue was getting back to normal after the four-day extravaganza, Mrs. McKenna made phone calls to newspapers that hadn't sent a reporter to cover her festival. She told them what a time they had missed and that they should be ashamed of themselves.

She remembered every grower for two hundred miles and every prize pumpkin that had ever slid onto the giant scale her father donated to the festival in 1953. Adelaide McKenna was a big woman of big gestures, and she walked the grounds like a queen touring her kingdom, kissing babies, tasting pies, and patting pumpkins. She did this pretty much at Grace's party, too.

Nana said Mrs. McKenna was a great community servant, but for my money no woman is truly great if her house has only one bathroom. The door finally opened and out scurried Justin Julee, the smallest boy in school, who had to sit on the Greater Des Moines white *and* yellow pages just to pass driver's ed.

I slipped inside and checked the damage. Richard was right: My eyes were clumpy. I tried peeling the mascara off, but the lashes stuck together, a look Wes wouldn't go for. I washed the remainder of a once-perfect makeup job off my face and considered spending the evening in the linen closet. But growing giant pumpkins had prepared me for life's bad weather: When it hit, you fought back, that's all.

I heard a knock on the door and Sharrell Upton's twinkling voice. "I just hate to be a pain, but I'm gonna have to get in there *soon!*"

Sharrell was the cheerleading cocaptain of the Rock River Belles and a Sweet Corn Coquette contestant. We weren't close. I opened the door to her *look,* which said she had to go bad. I lingered at the door making small talk, so she'd have to hold it longer. Sharrell had Bambi eyes with long, curly lashes that didn't clump, and a small waist that she always put one hand on for emphasis. Since I couldn't be the prettiest girl at the party I could at least make it uncomfortable for the one who was.

Sharrell was about to lose it and flung herself toward the toilet. I crept toward the living room, positioning myself behind Mrs. McKenna's plastic palm, which I had never seen any use for until now. I felt common and ugly. A fungus in a land of flowers.

Richard would never hide behind a fake tree. He was in the thick of it, talking to two soccer players about how Iowa needed a professional baseball team. The soccer players could clearly care less, but Richard's feeling was if people didn't like baseball, tough. The boys were looking at the pretty girls, who were pretending not to notice. Sharrell entered like no big deal that everyone was watching her. Just once I would like to walk into a room and have people notice. Was that too much to ask, God? I threw my braid over my left shoulder and tossed Mother's earrings for effect. Mrs. McKenna's clammy hand was on my shoulder, jingling with gold bracelets.

"Ellie dear, why don't you have something to eat?"

"I'm sort of on a diet."

"Nonsense," she said, and dragged me to a table of food that bulged with empty calories. I chucked my diet, cut a giant wedge of butter pecan cake, and dug in. Grace ran up to me and pointed to Wes, who was dressed in jeans and a work shirt and leaning against the fireplace, talking to a group of kids in fancier clothes. Seeing him put a knot in my stomach. Was I ready for *the* introduction?

"No," I told her, scarfing down cake and holding in my stomach (not easy, trust me). "I'm not."

Grace pulled me to the fireplace, yanked Wes's elbow, and announced to him and the world: "This is Ellie. You know. The one with the pumpkin."

This was not the quiet introduction Grace had promised. Wes and I looked at each other uncomfortably as the others smirked. I had never thought of myself as the One with the Pumpkin. I had other qualities I felt Grace could have brought out. The One with the Gift for Growing, the One with the Pretty Good Skin, the One with a Deep Love and Respect for Nature. I checked my upper lip for frosting. Wes smiled at me. I had never seen him close up before. He was not handsome really, but had very nice gray eyes. He grinned wider and said he'd heard about Max.

"He's big," I said.

"Yeah. I heard."

This was my usual brilliant beginning when I

talked to a boy. I can never think of anything interesting to say, so I keep going, hoping he won't notice.

"He's almost four hundred pounds by now so, you know, he could really be something, maybe, or it could all go away. You know."

"How could it all go away?" he asked.

I didn't know why I said that. Sometimes I was afraid I'd wake up and Max would be gone. "Gypsies," I offered. "Nuclear war." Wes laughed, not out of politeness. I laughed back.

"Do you think they'll drop the bomb on Des Moines?" he joked. He was leaning against the fireplace, looking directly at me. He was cute close up.

I laughed some more and was feeling pretty good even though my face was bare. I made Mother's earrings tinkle as I talked and could feel my eyes sparkle. I put my hand on my waist for emphasis, not because Sharrell did it but because it was the right thing to do. We talked about corn, how Texas A&M had developed a sweet onion with a taste nobody could believe, and some things that didn't matter. I went numb. Wes's eyes crackled and didn't miss a thing. He told me how his aunt had grown a 481-pound squash, the biggest one he'd ever met personally.

"It took my father and three other men to lift it onto the truck," he remembered. "They wrapped it in blankets, and my aunt rode all the way to the fair in the back with it because she said if it broke, she'd die. Won first prize."

"I'm hoping to enter," I said, humbly.

"Enter? Just enter? What about *winning*?"

Well, of course I wanted to win. You don't go entering contests you don't hope to win. "Cyril Pool's got one bigger than mine already," I said, "and he's been at this much longer than me and . . ." I stopped because I hated it when I put myself down around people I wanted to like me. I wanted to tell him how important Max was to me. How I'd covered him in the storm all night and given him the best months of my life, and how I had, as Nana said, a grower's soul.

"I'd like to win," I said quietly.

Wes looked at me like he was angry. "Well, what are you going to do to make yours bigger? What are you going to do to win?" He said "win" like it was everything.

I was defensive now: "I'm going to water him, and feed him, and—"

"Well, don't you think this Cyril's going to do that, too?"

Of course I knew that. I was three-time winner of the Rock River Young Growers' Competition. I hadn't seen him up there collecting any ribbons for giant corn. I could smell the Tide detergent on his lumberjack shirt and gulped. He was sizing me up, and I was acting like a loser.

"Ellie," he said leaning closer, "you've gotta do something more than this Cyril would ever think about or have the guts to do."

"I've got guts. Plenty of guts."

Wes scooped a carrot curl from a nearby plate, pointed it in the air, and watched me like he was trying to figure something out.

"You've got to have guts to grow giant pumpkins," I declared. "And heart." I thumped mine. "I've got a lot of heart."

I took a carrot curl and pointed it in response, waiting for him to tell me what Cyril wouldn't have the guts to do. His eyes were far off now. He wasn't talking.

"Are you going to tell me?" I asked.

"I'm thinking." His eyes narrowed. "I just met you and don't know if you can handle it."

I'm getting mad now because I've already invested a lot in this relationship and this guy is playing games. I've got better things to do than stand here holding this carrot curl and sucking in my stomach.

"Listen," I said, "I'm sixteen years old and I've grown five three-hundred-plus pounders, so don't go telling me what I can handle."

That was a gamble, but definitely the right thing to say because Wes's face broke into a grin. He motioned me forward and whispered: "You've got to talk to it."

I waited for more, but there wasn't any. He ate his carrot curl. I ate mine. "That's it," he said. "That's the secret."

"Talk to it," I repeated, and he looked at me like *he* was the champion grower and I was a hack.

"It's *your* pumpkin, Ellie. You grew it. You've got to talk to it. My aunt Izzy talked to hers every day and it just popped out. Never seen such a thing. She patted it, you know? Treated it just like she wanted people to treat her."

"I talk to it." I said this quietly because you never knew who was listening.

"How?" Wes challenged. Thought he was big stuff, this guy, a real control freak.

How? I didn't know how, I just did. Sometimes I'd say "Good morning," but mostly I beamed messages to Max's core. I didn't talk to him like he was a person because my feelings went deeper than that. So I said, "We communicate. Trust me," and was going to change the subject to corn and the American farmer.

"You probably think I'm crazy," Wes said.

Yes, I did. And pushy. "No," I lied.

"I mean *really* talk to it. You know . . . like a mother talks to a baby," he explained, getting real emotional now. "Have you seen what they do, new mothers?"

I hadn't been living in a cave all these years. I had read my mother's journal straight through four times and understood this total devotion. "I've seen mothers with babies," I assured him.

He was on another planet now: "They take the baby and cuddle it and talk to it and tell it everything they're doing and how much they love it. The little kid lies there and soaks up all that attention. Well, my aunt Izzy did that with two of her pumpkins and three of her children. She even read to those pumpkins out in the field—told them about herself—what she was aiming to do with them, the whole nine yards. And I swear, those pumpkins heard her and did what she said."

I wanted to excuse myself and go somewhere to breathe because something about this guy made me very nervous. He had a real grower's soul and wasn't afraid to show it. I'd never seen that in anyone my age. When he talked he used his hands big and wide. There was energy coming out of him that scared me to death. He understood the land, probably never wanted to be anything else but a farmer, year after year, working the earth. Suddenly the most important thing in my life was standing right there and not moving.

"Do you know how to do this?" I asked. "This talking thing?"

"Oh, yeah," he said, smiling. "I sure do."

Mrs. McKenna was passing around a bowl of peanuts, breaking into everyone's conversations, asking,

"Would you like a peanut, dear?" I took one, hoping she'd go away. I tried to crack it open ladylike, but the shell wouldn't budge. I forced the top off, tossed the nuts to my mouth, missed, and with Wes watching, dropped the whole thing down my blouse. I stood there frozen, pretending it didn't happen. Wes looked at his shoes, I looked at my shoes. We looked at everything except each other, which was just as well, because my face was burning red. The peanut shell started itching you know where, and I didn't want to leave because I didn't want to give up my place near Wes, who was talking again about his aunt's squash because there wasn't anything else to do.

"And when she finally cut into it," he explained into the carpet, "the meat wasn't tough like most Big Maxes'. It was sweet, you couldn't believe it."

The peanut was scratching and moving. I pretended to cough to shake it free but it just lodged deeper as Wes went on and on about talking to vegetables, which sounded like it would take some practice to get good at.

"Have you hugged your pumpkin today?" I offered.

"Right," Wes said.

The shell was burrowing in deep now. I tried a queer little hop and a twist while coughing to loosen it, which didn't work either. It was itching bad and growing to the size of a goiter. Soon I would need surgery. I excused myself, ran down the hall, and prayed that God would punish anyone who tried to take my place.

The line at the bathroom was two deep, which would have pleased Mrs. McKenna, who maintained that one bathroom promoted family unity. The facts were not in her favor. Her two oldest daughters married men in the plumbing business and moved out of town.

I found a closet, inched inside, and brushed the peanut remains from my chest—scarred for life. I shook myself to get any particles off, and cracked the door. Mr. McKenna was hiding in the hall, smoking his pipe. Mr. McKenna manufactured grain elevators and never knew what to say to a roomful of teenagers, so the hall was a pretty good place for him. I liked Mr. McKenna because he knew who he was and didn't try to be someone else. Being an elevator man, he respected a person's privacy.

He was puffing away in his favorite corner, his face fogged by smoke, in direct sight of my closet. Wes's laugh rose from the living room, and I knew I had to go for it. I walked from the closet; Mr. McKenna lowered his pipe in surprise.

"Ellie," he said. "You were in the closet."

"Yes, sir." I saw no use lying.

He considered this. "Everything . . . all right?"

I smiled. "Yes, sir. You know how it is."

Mr. McKenna did indeed, dug his heels into his corner, and resumed puffing. I moved toward the living room and Wes's laugh. JoAnn Clark grabbed me.

"You'd better get in there!" she whispered, pushing me ahead.

"What?"

"Just walk over like you belong there and don't panic."

"What are you talking about?" I asked.

JoAnn looked at me like I was a baby animal alone in the wild, and pointed to the living room just beyond the plastic palm. There stood Wes, laughing as big and wide as the whole outdoors, and at his elbow wiggled Sharrell, probably the next Sweet Corn Coquette, batting her eyes, gazing up at him. Sharrell, with her perfect makeup and tiny waist, who couldn't fertilize her way out of a starter box. In *my* place!

I backed from the scene, stunned.

"Listen," said JoAnn, "just go over there and—"

"I *can't!*"

"Yes, you can. Just test it, you know? I'll go with you and—"

I ran from the room, my eyes stinging, past Mr. McKenna and his cloud of smoke, past the closet, and into the bathroom, which was, mercifully, empty. Where the evening had begun.

Chapter
Five

I **sat on the McKennas' soft** pink toilet seat remembering the messages from Dad's motivational tapes on success, inner strength, and self-esteem. He had drilled them into me two years ago hoping I would become a different person. It didn't work.

The trick was to repeat positive phrases about yourself until you believed them even if they were lies, which they usually were: "I look forward to each new day with anticipation and joy." "I believe in myself. I really do."

There were fifty phrases on each tape; Dad said it took a normal person thirty days for the messages to really sink in—longer if you were a total loser.

"I am an interesting person," I quoted from memory. "My life has worth and meaning. I enjoy my life." I twisted a pink Kleenex into a gruesome shape and stood before the towel rack gritting my teeth as positive reprogramming messages filled my mind. "I look forward to each new day with anticipation and love for all humanity." I shook with frustration, beating the towel rack with my Kleenex. "I respond to life's challenges with hope and determination. I am not afraid of change, for it is change that makes me stronger."

I was whipping the tissue now, pounding the soap dish. So much for strength and hope. "I believe in myself," I growled. "I enjoy being me." The Kleenex was mangled and shredded. Wes and Sharrell were together, probably in love, and planning their wedding. "I will deal with this like a reasonable person," I shrieked. "I will not forsake reason for emotion. I will kick Sharrell in her flat little stomach and enjoy being me. I really will!"

I stomped the Kleenex to death and flushed it down Mrs. McKenna's happy pink toilet.

Richard wouldn't have let this happen to him. He was always in charge. When Dad passed out his WHERE I WANT TO BE IN TEN YEARS AND HOW I'M GOING TO GET THERE goal cards at the Rotary Club dinner for promising young athletes, Richard knew exactly where he wanted to be. Center field at Wrigley Field. In twenty-five years? The Baseball Hall of Fame in Cooperstown, New York. Richard made the best of things because for him there was always another game. Luck follows you when you're a partial baseball star. Life gives you breaks. When you grow giant pumpkins you sit on a lot of soft pink toilet seats, believe me.

An angry crowd was gathering outside the bathroom. I walked out, head high, and knew what any grower worth her salt must do when faced with an insect like Sharrell messing up her garden. The only way to deal with bugs is all-out attack. But before you spray, you've got to identify them.

There's a professor at the University of Massachusetts who is the greatest insect specialist in the entire country probably. You can send him a bug, in a crushproof container, that's bothering your garden or you, and he will tell you more than you'd ever want to know about the thing for $12.50. I didn't think I had a crushproof container big enough to shove Sharrell into, so as far as identifying her went, I was on my own.

Bugs never attack a garden without reason, and I figured Sharrell didn't, either. She could handpick any boyfriend she wanted, so her interest in Wes didn't figure. It was plain he was not her type and that they'd make each other *and* me miserable. Wes did not play football, or have a varsity sweater or a thick neck. His clothes weren't with it, his truck was ten years old, and I'd bet this month's allowance he'd never danced a step in his life. I watched them from the hall, trying to read lips. It didn't work. I decided to crash the party.

JoAnn saw me, and being my absolute best friend plus a great eavesdropper, walked with me to Wes and Sharrell's cozy corner. Sharrell was fluttering the lashes of her Bambi eyes, and Wes had a gooey look on his face.

Eavesdropping was something JoAnn and I got good at when her older sister, Beth, still lived at home and necked with her boyfriend at every opportunity. We learned a lot about life that year, not as much as Beth, but enough to keep things interesting. JoAnn grew African violets and had a sensitive grower's ear that picked up conversations from across a noisy room. She plugged into Wes and Sharrell like a ham radio operator.

"It's not bad," JoAnn said, stroking her ear for better volume. "They're talking about corn. What it's used for, how it grows, you know."

Now, my experience with romance has been, so far, slim. But that hasn't kept me from thinking about it. I knew that when a boy and a girl got cuddly the subject would not be corn.

"This is very bizarre," JoAnn said, watching her prey. "She's really pumping him about corn, Ellie. What's she up to?"

We looked at each other and suddenly knew. Sharrell Upton, who had won every beauty title in Rock River from the age of six, was a favored contestant for the coveted title of Sweet Corn Coquette. The winner got a thousand-dollar savings bond and a two-hundred-dollar gift certificate at Loward's Department Store plus all that adulation. And what would impress the judges most during the agricultural questioning?

"Why do you want to be Sweet Corn Coquette?" the judges always asked each contestant. A sampling of former winners' answers showed a misunderstanding of corn and its merits:

"Because I think it's a wonderful vegetable, Your Honor."

"Because sweet corn makes me proud to be an American."

"Because corn is . . . well . . . gee . . . it's juicy and practical."

This part of the contest always gave growers a big hoot, but a contestant who could answer thoughtfully *and* look great in a yellow chiffon dress would be a shoo-in. Sharrell held on to Wes's arm like it was the first ear of the season. I plotted my attack.

"How's it going?" It was Richard.

"Great. Really great."

Richard cleared his throat, picked an orange from a fruit bowl, and slapped it into his left hand over and over, like a baseball. "So," said Richard, watching Wes and Sharrell in the corner.

I looked at JoAnn, who shrugged, meaning they were still talking corn. It hadn't occurred to Wes, I'm sure, that corn and pumpkins were both native American vegetables and simply went together because God had planned it that way. Ask any Wampanoag (or was it Sioux?)—he was eating corn and pumpkins and doing just fine for hundreds of years before those sneaky Europeans arrived, who were probably Sharrell's relatives. Ask any Pilgrim how he survived the first long, cold winter. Corn and pumpkins—that's what he'll tell you. You can't fight nature. Or destiny.

This gave me hope, and I was feeling pretty smug with centuries of agricultural heritage behind me. Sharrell had no right to take my place. I stormed the gates, sat down next to Wes, looked Sharrell dead on, and sprayed.

"So, Sharrell," I said, feeling my seams tighten, "how's the beauty contest business?"

"Whatever do you mean?" said she.

"I mean the Sweet Corn Coquette contest. You have entered, haven't you?"

Sharrell was smiling like a big fake and Richard was inching closer. I jangled Mother's earrings for strength and twirled my braid.

"Well, of course I've entered."

"What," asked Wes, amused, "is a Sweet Corn Coquette?"

"It's the very highest honor for beauty contestants," Sharrell said. "The Sweet Corn Coquette represents corn farmers in the entire region."

"Doing what?" Wes continued.

"Whatever do you mean?"

"How," asked Wes, "does a Sweet Corn Coquette represent corn farmers in the region?"

"Well . . ." She was floundering. "By making appearances . . . by smiling, you know . . ."

"Smiling," said Wes.

"And waving," Sharrell continued. "From floats and things. And we eat corn, of course, at the dinners and festivals, but without butter, so it won't slop down your dress. That's a little contest secret." She giggled.

Wes was watching Sharrell strangely, maybe seeing the light. "I always wondered what those contests were like," I said. "How do you enter?"

Sharrell shook her mane of corn-blond hair: "I just filled out a little card and—"

"I think," said Richard, joining in, "what we want to know is what are the qualifications? Do you have to be a grower or at least know something about corn to represent the farmers?"

"Well," she said, batting her eyes, "they never asked *me* any of that."

"Ah," said Richard, flipping his orange, "I know something about corn."

"Probably not as much as Wes here," Sharrell purred.

"Probably not," Richard agreed, "but probably more than a Sweet Corn Coquette contestant."

"Oh, I wouldn't be so sure," she snapped. "Wes's been teaching me real good."

Richard smiled and held his orange out like a microphone: "Two questions, Sharrell, and the Sweet Corn Coquette crown can be yours." A small crowd had gathered, mostly of average-looking girls who hated Sharrell's guts.

"Question number one," he shouted. "When is corn

planted? Please think before you answer." Richard checked his watch as Sharrell, not knowing, wiggled in embarrassed silence.

"Time's up," said Richard, turning to the crowd. "Does anyone know the answer?"

"Spring!" shouted several people in unison.

"Correct," said Richard. "Spring. Remember that, Sharrell. It's important to know when corn is planted if you're going to wave from floats and represent corn farmers in the entire region. Now for question number two: Why do *you* want to be this year's Sweet Corn Coquette? Please think before you answer."

Sharrell stood in fury. "I don't have to take this!" she cried, and stormed off.

"Correct!" Richard shouted. "Because she doesn't have to take this."

The kids laughed appreciatively. Wes shook his head in disbelief. Richard walked away peeling his orange like a pitcher who had just nailed a no-hitter. Wes and I were on the couch by Mrs. McKenna's plastic palm, alone, the closest I had ever sat to a boy in my whole life. I felt wonderful, then ugly, and definitely guilty.

"I guess that was mean," I said.

Wes shrugged, looking at his shoes. They were good farmer's shoes—old, practical, caked with mud.

"She'll probably win," I said. "She always does."

"And represent the great American corn farmer?"

It was my turn to shrug. "Somebody has to. I guess."

"Nobody has to," said Wes, looking right at me.

I wanted to tell him that I understood and forgave him, that growers take pride in being independent and don't go outside for help or understanding even when they really need it. I knew he loved nature and didn't need flash. The closest bond we had was the soil, and there was plenty of that on his shoes.

"My grandparents were farmers," I said.

"Mine, too."

"My father skipped the line and left the growing to me," I explained, not sure why I wanted him to know that.

"Yeah, my dad hated farming, too," Wes said. "He's a sales manager. That's why we moved up here. I didn't like it in the beginning, but it's not so bad. It kind of grows on you."

It does indeed.

Dad, of course, was at the McKennas' at exactly eleven o'clock, when the party ended. The first parent there. Wes was talking to Grace when Dad shoved Richard and me out the door. We waved good-bye, and Grace winked at me, meaning she would get the low-down on everything and talk to me tomorrow.

The sky was clear, black, and filled with stars— the kind of sky I remembered as a child when Dad would wake me up to see the constellations in perfect display. Dad gave me his love for stars. It was the only part that stuck with him from his life on the farm. Dad said he would lie out in the fields as a boy, counting stars trillions of miles out in space. He had an astronomy club with four other boys. They called themselves the Knights of the Night, a totally uncool name, but one of the boys became a space engineer at NASA. You never know how nerds are going to turn out.

Richard, Dad, and I stood on Mrs. McKenna's lawn, hushed under the stars, taking time to get our eyes used to the darkness. Dad's eyes searched the night sky like he was trying to solve a mystery. We found the October constellation Pegasus, the Flying Horse. It had four bright stars at the corners. Dad counted eighteen faint stars inside its square. Richard said the sky reminded him of a baseball stadium at night—high praise. I remembered Dad telling me to pick the star I wanted and it would be mine. As a child, I never believed that could happen, but tonight I felt lucky. I pointed to a small star hanging left of the McKennas' chimney and took ownership.

Dad laughed, opened the car door for me, and helped me inside. "Good party?" he asked hopefully as we sped off.

Richard said something about the greatness of Mrs. McKenna's butter pecan seven-layer cake. I said "Mmmmm," and looked out the window. My star was following us. It waited over Richard's house as we dropped him off, then trailed us home. I had picked well.

"Well," Dad said, "I'm sure the boys were buzzing around you tonight."

I laughed and blushed sort of, because he had never said that to me before. I walked out back to Max.

"Do you mind, Dad? I just need to—"

"Ellie," he sighed, "it's late now and—"

"Five minutes, okay?"

He sighed in defeat and went inside.

I crouched near Max and checked his runoff ditch, my khaki slacks pushing at the seams. I wondered where Wes was, what he was thinking about. I lifted the reemay cloth off, touched his skin, and in honor of the evening, gave it a go.

"Listen," I whispered. "It's me. Ellie." I felt dumb

doing this, but Wes had trusted me with his family secret because he knew I had guts. "I want you to know, Max, that I'm proud of how strong you are." I couldn't think of more to say so I squatted there as Max soaked that in. "I know you can do it, Max," I continued, "because you're a champion. It's important you know that because you're going to have to stretch a little more so we can beat the daylights out of Cyril Pool at the Weigh-In, who is thirty-five and a world-class sludge."

My star hung over us, which I really appreciated, because the next part was not as easy to say. "Not meaning to bring up negatives, Max, but Cyril's pumpkin's a deep orange color, deeper than you. Not that you're not great-looking, you understand, and granted, weight's the thing they go by, but you do look sort of pale. Good color just makes the whole win more dramatic, so if you could work on that, too, I'd appreciate it. Think orange, Max. Big, bright, and orange. Got it?"

I stood up, and my pants ripped completely across the seam. It was inevitable, but for once in my life, my timing had been decent.

Chapter Six

I t was **Sunday,** 7:00 A.M., eight hours after Dad had dragged me from the Party of the Year, and Grace still hadn't called to report on Wes. I had called the McKennas' house fifteen minutes earlier, figuring they'd be awake since the sun was, after all, up. They weren't.

I called JoAnn Clark, who I knew would be up—people who grow African violets sleep lightly. We decided that Wes, being of good farm stock, had probably been awake for hours walking the fields, thinking about what a delightful girl I was and what a deadhead Sharrell really was—and he'd never even seen me with my perfect makeup job. I made Dad coffee and baking powder cheese biscuits, of which I was determined to eat only two bites. Cheese biscuits made Dad feel loved and appreciated, which kept him peaceful during breakfast. The Rock River Pumpkin Weigh-In and Harvest Fair was twenty breakfasts away, and you can bet my father was going to be swimming in warm, cheesy heaven.

Dad was attacking one of his Important Life Goals: running seven miles in under forty minutes. He'd trimmed his speed down to forty-two minutes, which I told him was a miracle for a person of his extreme age. He flopped in the kitchen dripping wet, checked his watch, and collapsed.

"It's conceivable," Dad said, wheezing, "that I could be dead."

I poured coffee into his "Forty Isn't Old If You're a Tree" mug and got myself a glass of water.

"You look tired," I said, being kind. Actually, Dad's face had that dark, craggy look that Abraham Lincoln got during the Civil War. Dad had added three new clients to his schedule last month, which meant he was working round the clock when he wasn't running. He wasn't sleeping well, either, but then, he hardly ever did.

"Maybe you should cut back, Dad."

Dad did not believe in the concept of rest. He closed his eyes, tensed his muscles, and breathed deeply.

"A harnessed mind," he said, "can change the body."

I considered my body and knew the only thing that would change it was basic starvation. He did severe stretching exercises to prove his point. I took the perfectly browned biscuits out of the oven and told my body it wasn't hungry. This concept didn't take. I ran from the kitchen a broken person, with a cheese biscuit clenched in my fist.

Everything went down the toilet in October (especially my grades) because pushing a winning squash to the limit took everything I had. Miss Moritz was pumping up for her fall extravaganza: "The Major Battles of

World War II and How They Make Us *Feel* Today." She wanted us to "connect with the emotion of the battle-field because history isn't just facts, it's *feelings*." My feelings for the battlefield weren't deep.

Dad didn't appreciate that the next twenty days were *the* most important in all of the pumpkin-growing competition. This was when a giant could gain ten pounds per day or die in rot, and then where were you? Out in the cold, that's where. Dad picked homework over squash nurturing every time. Cyril Pool didn't have this pressure. Cyril did have stupidity working against him, which gave me hope, since Cyril didn't even know he was stupid.

It was 7:32. Grace still hadn't called to tell me about Wes. I checked the phone to make sure it was working. Maybe Grace's phone wires had been cut by terrorists.

Now it was 7:47. The smell of Dad's remaining biscuits filled the house, and I picked off another one. I tried the phone line three minutes later, when three gunshots sounded in the distance. Gunshots weren't heard in Rock River except when the VFW went duck hunting, which they never did on Sunday. This could be trouble.

Dad and I ran outside. More gunshots were blast-ing. An old truck sped around the corner. It was pur-sued by Mannie Plummer in her gingham housecoat, holding a rifle screeching fire. "They took it!' she screamed, pointing down Bud DeWitt Memorial Drive. "They stole it right in plain daylight! They stole my baby!"

Roxye and Phil Urice came out of their house be-cause Mannie had flopped down on their lawn in her grief and they had just fertilized it real good yesterday morning. Mannie didn't notice, and Roxye and Phil weren't about to tell her. Mrs. Lemming stuck her head out her front door, saw Mannie slumped on the newly fertilized lawn, and within minutes waddled down the street with a jug of cider and paper cups, which she passed out to the small crowd that had gathered. Mannie was crying bad, the first casualty of the season. Roxye went to call the police, but it wouldn't do any good.

"I'm too old to have another one," Mannie groaned, cradling her rifle, which Phil took gently from her. She was sixty-five, her back was giving out, and we all knew she was right.

Mrs. Lemming said it was such a shame, such a waste; Roxye said the sheriff was on his way and they'd had one taken earlier this morning at Gloria Shack's farm—a three-hundred-pounder.

"Mine weighed two hundred and some," Mannie sobbed. "My biggest yet."

This was a rough break for Mannie. Her parakeet had croaked three months earlier and she was just getting back to enjoying life. We were quiet out of respect for her loss, but fear gripped my heart at the thought that terrorized every giant-pumpkin grower in the area. The pumpkin thieves had begun their murderous ride! They could strike anywhere, anytime, slashing vines, lifting helpless giants from their homes. Out-of-town department stores bought, schools bought, lesser harvest festivals bought, and selfish millionaires on country estates that just wanted the pumpkins for themselves. The going rate was $1.10 a pound. Nobody, it seemed, could stop the thieves. I wondered if they had Cyril's address.

But Max! I hugged Mannie hard and ran back

home, leaving Dad with the thing he loved most: a group that needed motivating.

Max sat safe and untouched in the garden, soaking up the morning sun. We'd been spared for now. I watered him well and checked for kidnappers. Two pumpkins snatched in one morning. This was bad, very bad.

"Did you see them, Max?" I whispered. "Did you see the bad men?"

Max couldn't give a description, but I had my suspicions, and they were all named Dennis. Dennis Hickey. A mean, hulky nineteen-year-old junior who flunked eighth grade three times and was passed on to Rock River High like the Asian flu when his five-o'clock shadow made his thirteen-year-old classmates so nervous they started calling him "sir." In high school, Dennis could not pass remedial freshman English, but managed to get his driver's license and a smelly old pickup that was just the right size for squash snatching. Last October Dennis had shown up at school waving a wad of money and cracking jokes about pumpkin pie.

Richard defended Dennis because they played on the same baseball team, and where baseball was concerned, Dennis was a good sport. He was also a good first baseman who growled at every runner he tagged, scaring some to their knees because he had three front teeth missing. I pointed out to Richard that Dennis also kicked bunnies and threw rocks at squirrels. He ate a caterpillar once on a bet, and spray-painted First Presbyterian Church's Christmas manger iridescent purple when the minister told him he was "not the right type" to play Joseph in the holiday pageant.

"He has a great arm," Richard said.

"Is that all that's important to you?" I shrieked. "He could be the pumpkin vandal, a serial killer! He's disgusting and grotesque. He burps and hates animals. He—"

"Bats .340," Richard said.

"How could someone so rotten at life in general be so good on a baseball field?" I hollered. Richard, the son of a praying Catholic woman, said, "It's a mystery," which for Catholics neatly covered life's unexplained mess. I was Presbyterian and hadn't been given as many answers. Richard said Dennis could not be the pumpkin vandal because Dennis wasn't smart enough.

"We'll see," I said.

"There's no way, Ellie."

"You don't have to be a genius to steal pumpkins."

"But," Richard said, "you have to have a plan. You have to *think* about it. You have to be motivated."

"I get your point."

Nobody gave pumpkin growers an inch. You could slave all season like poor Mannie Plummer and have your prize vegetable end up in some window next to a mannequin decked out for Halloween. Two years ago, Helen Bjork's 294-pounder was stolen, and she swears she saw it in the window of a florist's in Ebberton. Dad wouldn't let me stay home for the next twenty days to guard Max, and since vegetable branding hadn't been perfected yet, I needed a plan.

It was 8:59. The phone rang. I raced inside. It was Grace. About time. I positioned myself to keep Max in sight. "Well," she began, "I talked to him for a long time after you left."

"And?"

"Well, he said he really liked the party and my friends." This was not heart-stopping news, and Grace always needed to tell the whole story before she got to the good part.

"Okay . . ." I said.

"Then he said he was having some trouble with his truck and had been fixing it all day. He likes trucks and things."

"Great," I said. He likes trucks. Does he like *me*?

"Um, he said his dog was sick and he had to take him to the vet because he'd been coughing. He was worried about him, getting used to a new vet and all, the dog's pretty old, and he wants to see your pumpkin."

"Say the last part again."

"He wants to see Max."

"At my house?" I was overcome.

"Well, yeah, where else?"

"Right," I said. Grace had finished. "Anything else, Grace?" I asked, my heart pounding. "I mean, did he say anything about me, you know?"

"Well, he said he liked Mom's butter pecan cake and that he hoped you won at the Weigh-In."

"He said that?"

Grace was jump-started now: "Yes, he did. And I could tell by his face, not that he said anything directly, you know, but his face said that he liked you. I could tell on account of we're cousins and I know him pretty well."

"But he didn't say anything about me personally."

"No, but I could tell."

"Maybe," I said, "I should invite him over next weekend to see Max. No. That's too forward and—"

"Not a good idea."

"No," I agreed.

"He's driving down to see his old girlfriend next weekend."

"But you said he liked me, that—"

"Those roads are bad, Ellie. Potholes, slow traffic. She's not that great."

"You've met her?"

"No," said Grace, "but I can tell."

Nana said she would guard Max from ten to two for the next few days while I was at school. I had rigged a jiggly fence around him with hanging bells that would ring if a pumpkin thief tried something sneaky. I painted a sign, BACK OFF, CREEPS, YOU'RE BE- ING WATCHED, and stuck it by the fence. Not state- of-the-art protection, but enough to get a robber to think twice. I hoped.

Rock River High was decorated in orange and brown crepe paper in honor of the upcoming fair, when all schools closed and children ran free. Mrs. Zugoruk's freshman art class had covered the bulletin boards with crepe paper cornucopias that looked like torna- does. The great pumpkin-pie-baking contest was on as Marsha Mott collected cans of puréed pumpkin for her mother, who promised to someday deliver a 350-pound pie, the world's largest, to the fair if it killed her. Marsha said it probably would, unless the family fin- ished her off first.

It was afternoon, and I hadn't seen Wes yet. In study hall I boned up on corn. Tossing a few corn facts in Wes's direction couldn't hurt, especially since he was visiting the Other One this coming weekend.

I was worried about Max because Nana couldn't sit him for the next nineteen days. I needed more than bells and threats for peace of mind. Cyril was probably sleeping in his field with a cannon. With any luck, Cyril would fire the thing and blow up his foot, or better yet,

Big Daddy. Richard suggested I get a guard dog to ward off vandals.

"One with a loud bark," Richard said, eating a school cafeteria meatball sandwich.

"I don't like dogs."

"They probably sense that," said Richard. "A dog will respond to you just the way you respond to him."

"I don't do dogs."

"It's like medicine," Richard explained. "You take it when you need it."

"Think of something else."

"There is nothing else, Ellie, that you can afford."

"A retired policeman—"

"Would have to be paid and would not sit in your field."

"A burglar alarm system—"

Richard looked at me with pity. "The wires could be cut, and if you try to skip school, Miss Moritz would have you arrested."

The last three years I had played fast and loose with my squashes, but Max was different, world-class. He was 450 pounds already, my biggest yet by 130 pounds, and still growing. "You think I need a guard dog," I groaned.

Richard ate a Ho-Ho. "Only for nineteen days."

The woman at the Rock River Dog Pound informed me that *her* dogs had been through enough, were absolutely *not* for rent, and that I should be ashamed of myself for asking. The woman at the pet store said *only* fish were refundable, and *only* if they died of natural causes within one week after purchase. A dog—she eyed me coldly—was forever. The woman at the office of Des Moines Adopt-a-Doggie said *her* dogs were sensitive and loving and only asked for a good home. Was that too much? If I wanted a "brash, unruly killer" I should call the police. The police said guard dogs were only used by trained professionals, and just what kind of business was I in anyway?

I had not seen Wes at all, which was bad because he could forget me even though I was unforgettable two nights before. A chill was in the air bringing more bad news. Thieves had stormed the countryside pilfering two pumpkins across the Rock River border in Ebberton. Four down in thirty-six hours. Doom fell upon every grower.

Richard showed up for dinner (split pea soup with sausage, biscuits, carrot salad, and sautéed cinnamon apples), dragging Spider, a large, bony mongrel in need of a bath.

"He has no teeth," I pointed out.

"Doesn't need them," Richard said, nodding to Spider, who wheezed and lay down on my clean kitchen floor. Spider eyed the basket of biscuits longingly, and me like I was flea spray. "Give him a biscuit," Richard directed.

"I'm not wasting one of my biscuits on a—"

Richard sighed, grabbed a biscuit, and placed it in my hand. "Give it to him, Ellie. Tell him he's a good dog." Spider glared at the biscuit in my hand, stood up, and started to growl. Spider was ugly but not stupid, and his *look* said to me that if he got the biscuit no one would get hurt. I threw it on the floor. He tossed it down, drooled, and crawled off to watch me by the back door.

"There," said Richard. "You're on your way."

"To what?"

"Peace of mind," he said, ladling pea soup into a bowl.

"Where is this dog from? What planet?" Spider was snoring now, insensitive to criticism.

"The Ankers let me borrow him because Mr. Anker fell off his roof and needs lots of quiet for the next three weeks, which is impossible with Spider here."

"Why is it impossible?" Richard smiled and shrugged. "Is there something you should tell me?" I continued. "No. Don't tell me. I'll tell you. I can't do this."

"Do you know why they call him Spider?" Richard asked.

"I don't want to know."

"You do want to know," Richard said, beaming, "because he might not look like much—"

"He looks like my worst nightmare."

"He's a pumpkin thief's worst nightmare," Richard said. "Positively deadly."

I regarded the pumpkin thief's worst nightmare: splotchy coat, tattered ears, sleeping death rattle. "He gums robbers to death?" I asked. "What if they bring biscuits?"

"Robbers don't bake," said Richard, adding salt to *my* soup. Spider turned, old and battered, and snorted.

"I don't like this dog."

"You don't like any dog, but for nineteen days, you can like *this* dog."

Spider was drooling, his tongue hanging from his mouth like a dead snake. "This dog," I continued, "does not make me feel protected, you know? He's lying there doing nothing. This is not the mighty guard dog who will protect Max against evil."

"He doesn't have to do anything yet," Richard explained.

"This is a job interview, Richard. The dog so far has growled, eaten a biscuit—"

"He likes your biscuits."

"—tracked filth and disease across my kitchen—"

"When's your father coming home?" Richard asked.

"Any minute now. Why?" Dad's car pulled in the driveway, and Richard grinned. Suddenly the dead heap that was Spider rose from its ashes. His eyes flashed hate and destruction, his bark took over great and full. I jumped up on the sink as Richard watched him like a proud father.

"Hates noise," Richard shouted happily over the barking. "Drives him crazy. Tell him he's a good dog." Spider had reeled into attack mode, snarling and spitting gloom. This did not seem like a good dog to me. Dad froze at the back door.

"Tell him!" Richard yelled as Spider thrashed the screen door, trying to get to Dad, who was holding a rake to protect himself.

"Ellie!" Dad shouted. "Are you all right?"

"Yes, sir!" Richard yelled back. "We're fine!"

I jumped from the sink and grabbed a biscuit. Spider turned toward me, growling and fierce. "Good dog," I lied. He cocked his old head and looked at the biscuit. "Good dog," I said, dropping the biscuit, which he devoured. "That's a very good dog."

Spider licked his gums and lay down by the sink. "He wants you to scratch him," Richard explained.

"Never."

"Scratch," ordered Richard. I did, behind his ears.

He closed his eyes happily and rolled over, indicating his stomach.

"Forget it, Spider. I don't know where you've been."

Dad entered, holding a trash can lid like a shield. "What," whispered Dad, "is *that?*"

"Insurance," said Richard, handing Dad a biscuit. "How was your day, Uncle Mitchell?"

"Safe," said Dad, eyeing Spider, who burped and nuzzled my arm. "Very safe."

"He can sleep in the shed outside," said Richard. "He won't leave the property. Hates noise, remember? Gotta go."

"Richard," I snapped, "this is not a good thing for me. This does not make me happy." Spider, however, was happy, gurgling at my feet. Richard backed away. I was doing fine, he said.

"See you, Uncle Mitchell," Richard said, and waved.

"Young man," shouted Dad, "you're not seriously leaving this . . . this—"

"Dog," said Richard, almost out the door.

"If you leave now," I threatened him, "I will injure you. You will never play baseball again, I swear!"

"Would someone," cried Dad, "please explain to me what that thing is doing in my house?"

"Ellie will," said Richard, grabbing two biscuits and closing the screen door quietly. "It's her dog."

"You're a dead man, Richard!" I shrieked, smiling at Spider to not get him nervous. "Good dog," I told him. "Nice dog." I tore after Richard, down the back porch steps, into the cold, past Max and his bells and my BACK OFF, CREEPS sign. Richard, the rat, was gone.

Spider stood in the doorway gumming a cookie Dad had thrown at him.

"Spider," I said, "this is Max." Spider seemed to take that in stride. I pointed to the shed. "And this," I chirped, "is *your* house." Spider growled, lowered his tail, and slunk back into the kitchen. It was going to be a long evening.

Chapter Seven

Dad, I, and the neighbors slept about seven minutes during Spider's first night patrol. We got four angry calls about barking and two angrier calls mentioning rat poison, and I baked another batch of biscuits at 2:00 A.M. to silence Spider, who responded to a squeaky truck on Bud DeWitt Memorial Drive by reaching his full barking potential. Dad offered him a store-bought English muffin, which he spat out.

Frost was in the air, putting Max in more danger. Most pumpkins can recover from a slight frost, but freezing meant the end. I gobbled six butterscotch cookies because of the stress, and covered Max with an electric blanket roped with extension cords that led up the back porch. By now his leaves were as big as elephant ears, his main vine as thick as Dad's arm. I measured his circumference from stem to nose around his fattest area: 153 inches. He was an awesome 490 pounds according to my pumpkin estimated weight chart.

Big feeders like Max took 120 days to mature, and I had timed it well; we had 12 days to go to the Weigh-In, and Max was bulging beyond my dreams. I felt the solid hardness of his shell, tucked the blanket tighter, and let the good warmth soak in.

I'd been talking to Max like Wes said, but it made me feel stupid. As a loyal reader of *Seventeen*, I tried to be sophisticated whenever possible, because you never knew who was watching. I'd read Max an article about whether guys like girls with makeup to broaden his scope and take the pressure off always just growing. The article said if you be yourself you don't have to worry about anything else. I told Max that he was a great champion and all he had to do was be himself, but under no circumstances was he to be any less than that. I thought it was tacky of Wes to tell Grace he wanted to see Max and then get sick, not even show up in school for three whole days, and leave me wondering about everything.

"Max," I said, pulling my coat tight and adjusting the blanket's heat. Talking to an electric blanket made me feel dumber, and Spider was yelping at every chipmunk that scurried by. "There are times in life, Max, when we need to gather every ounce of strength and courage and move forward despite the odds." I got this speech from Richard, who got it from Mr. Soboleski, who got it in part from Vince Lombardi, who probably got it from Winston Churchill.

A cold wind whooshed from the north, and Max shivered. Normally I did not give orders to squashes and was known for giving my vegetables a lot of rope. But this cold was coming in quick even though the farm report had predicted a gentle, warm evening. Nana taught me not to rely on weather people because they don't have the good sense to stand outside and see what's happening.

"You will," I shouted, "*not* freeze, Max! You will think warm, think victory! You must be a man!"

Spider shrieked as Mrs. Lemming took her nightly bag of trash across the street and put it in the Urices' garbage can to fool the raccoon that had been driving her crazy for twenty years. Nana told her that raccoons don't live that long, but Mrs. Lemming said *hers* did and had been sent to earth to torment her all her days. She'd tried leaving a light on, but that hadn't worked. Neither had a radio. I turned up the heat for Max as Spider yelped through the quiet night.

Morning came quickly and Max made it through, toasty and safe, a tribute to Sommerset Electric and Dad's motivating powers. I grabbed Richard by the scruff of the neck when he dared to show up for breakfast. "I will kill you," I promised. Richard threw Spider a Snickers bar, which he devoured.

"He's got to go," I said.

"This," said Richard, scratching behind Spider's ears, "is the National Guard, Ellie."

"You left me alone with him."

"Your father was here, and Max," Richard said, "*is* still here. Just in case you haven't heard, another pumpkin bit the dust last night."

"Where?"

"Somewhere in Circleville. That's all I know."

The pumpkin thieves were everywhere now. Uncontrollable. I looked at Spider like the last woman on earth would look at the last man on earth even though he was Elmer Fudd. I adjusted.

"He has a nice face," I said as Richard and Spider nodded.

But getting Old Abe to see the light was another story. Dad's dark circles were deepening. I told Dad he could rise above adversity and attack one of his Important Life Goals: Beating Insomnia. Dad said Spider gave insomnia new meaning and had set a deadline: 6:00 P.M. No more Spider. The dog, sensing a biscuit-free future, licked my hand and curled up at my feet. He wasn't fooling anybody; still this was the first animal who had shown an interest in me. Spider put his paw in my hand. Contact! I stroked it like Annie Sullivan breaking through to Helen Keller.

"You are here to protect Max from bad people," I instructed. Spider panted in response. "I will bake you biscuits *if* you obey. That's the rule." Spider took this in, not as happily, and snarled. I held a biscuit over his head.

"Take it or leave it, pal." He lay down in defeat. "Another thing," I said. "You are making my father nervous. And he doesn't need outside help, if you get my meaning."

Dad appeared, inching toward the back door, shielded with his trash can lid, whispering, "Good dog. That's a good dog." I decided to go for the direct approach.

"I've got to keep him, Dad. I need you to understand."

"Ellie," he whispered, "this animal is a terror. Good dog, Spider."

"It's only for nineteen days—"

"That," Dad spat, "is interminable. Whole wars have been fought in less time."

"Like the Six-Day War," Richard offered, pleased with himself until I kicked him in the shin. "May I take that back, sir?" he asked, rubbing his leg.

"You may take this animal back."

"I can't do that, Uncle Mitchell."

Dad gave him a *look* that said this better be good. It was.

"Because, sir, Mr. Anker needs total quiet and bed rest and Mrs. Anker is pretty strung out, not to mention that Mrs. Anker's son broke his leg last month and can't get around too well, and anyway, I promised." Dad waited as Richard went for the big finish. "And, sir, not that this would matter to you, but Mrs. Anker's brother is head of Loward's Department Store, and she said she's never been in a place where the salespeople needed more motivating. And I'm sure that Mrs. Anker would mention this good deed you and Ellie are doing for old Spider here to her brother, who would maybe be interested in all that motivational stuff you do for companies."

Richard watched Dad and waited. He knew Dad had been gunning for Loward's Department Store (the biggest in the five-town area) as a client for two years and had hit nothing but a brick wall.

Dad harrumphed.

Spider caught a fly with his tongue. Deadly.

"If," Dad said, "you keep him outside, Ellie, then—"

"I will, Dad. I promise."

"And," Dad continued as Spider watched, sensing doom, "this constant racket must stop. You must discipline him, Ellie, to behave that way only to—"

"Pumpkin thieves," I said.

"Precisely," Dad agreed, glaring at Spider, who glared back. "He is only a dog, Ellie, and you are an intelligent, educated, enlightened person. Take control."

"I'll try, Dad."

Dad walked out the back door and turned to Richard. "Say hello to Mrs. Anker for me, will you?"

"I will do that, Uncle Mitchell, yes." A car horn beeped in the distance and Spider went nuts, growling and shaking at the hated sound. Dad, an intelligent, educated, enlightened person, threw a biscuit at Richard who caught it like a line drive and grounded it straight into Spider's mouth. Dad crawled out the door, not looking back.

Dennis was late to Miss Moritz's class, looking like he'd slept in his truck, which he probably had, typical of a crummy pumpkin thief. He came in during our re-enactment of Patton's march into Palermo and got to his seat just as Sicily (portrayed by the Bomgarten twins) fell noisily across three desks and crashed on the floor in defeat. Miss Moritz, her forehead perspiring with enthusiasm, asked how *this* major battle made us feel. I said it made me feel glad I wasn't in Italy, which a large portion of the class agreed with, including Joey Bongioriano and Gina Carlucci. Dennis yawned and blew his nose on his sleeve.

Miss Moritz wasn't happy with my answer or my grades. She did not understand the importance of champion squash training and its effect on lesser life issues such as homework. Miss Moritz wrote a note to Dad with the worst news possible: I was not working up to my full potential. That's all he needed.

"Ellie!" he boomed. "*What* is this?"

I looked at the stationery in his hand and took a wild guess. "A note, Dad?"

"An edict, young woman!"

Good study habits, he barked, were the road to

success in life, *not* growing pumpkins. Consistency brought rewards, *not* kneeling in the dirt watering an oversized gourd. World history was a pathway to truth, justice, and the American way.

"You will study," Dad informed me. "You will think clearly and resonantly. You will concentrate on your schoolwork first. Then and only then may you concentrate on that"—he struggled to form the word—"vegetable."

Between Spider's barking and Dad's edict, poor Max was surely shrinking inside. Richard had almost measured Cyril's pumpkin on the sly, but Cyril ran from his toolshed waving a lead pipe, and Richard took off. He said he couldn't tell how big it was, but that I should probably be nervous.

"I'm not nervous," I lied.

"Good," said Richard. "Be positive against the odds. Makes it easier to get out there on the mound."

I left Spider in the yard to guard Max and went to see for myself. Cyril's cousin, Herman, was guarding Big Daddy with a rifle. Herman looked like a squash with small, buggy eyes. Big Daddy looked like he belonged on a recruitment poster for growers. I was dead. Herman grinned and spat, never much for conversation.

I stared at the soon-to-be winning entry of this year's Rock River Pumpkin Weigh-In and Harvest Fair, my heart sinking to the earth's roots. "Well, Missy," cackled Cyril, coming up behind me, "whatcha gonna do with all that second-place money?"

This was Cyril's first stab at irony. Second-place money was fifty dollars and whatever you could get if you sold your seeds, which could be a lot, but I was never one for passing secrets outside the family.

The Weigh-In winner got it all: fame, respect, a dollar a pound, and his picture in the *Rock River Clarion*. The loser got left behind in the dust. "Don't spend it all in one place, now," Cyril continued, winking at Herman, who thought this was so hysterical he dropped his rifle on his toe.

"Say, Cyril," I shouted, trying to get even, "that *thing*—Big Daddy. Is he solid or full of rot like people say?"

"Ain't gonna work, Missy," Cyril shot back. I looked at gargantuan Big Daddy and knew he was right.

I walked off because school was starting soon— head down, hope gone—past Big Daddy, down Backfarb Road, across Bud DeWitt Memorial Drive, right into Rock River High, and smack into Wes and his clarinet case.

"Hi," Wes said.

"Oh," I said, feeling dumb. "Hi."

"You look strange."

I hadn't seen Wes for four days because he'd been sick and had hoped for a more thrill-packed moment. I looked at him. "Ellie," he continued, "are you okay?"

Cyril was going to stick it to me again and I was going to have to grin like a trained monkey at the fair and be a good sport and pretend that the most important thing to me didn't matter.

"Ellie," Wes repeated, "are you okay?"

Dennis was stealing squashes, and nobody knew it except me. He'd probably dupe Spider with biscuits and snatch Max and my life would be over. I looked at Wes and his gray eyes, framed by the harvest festival decorations in the school hall. He was wearing a denim work shirt and jeans that made him look taller. He was probably still in love with The Other One in Gaithersville and not even man-eating potholes could keep him from driving to her this weekend.

Was I okay?

"Ellie," he started again. At least he remembered my name.

"No," I said, flopping against the wall. "I'm not."

Wes was good about listening, having heard, of course, about the pumpkin thieves and their dirty, rotten ways. He said Spider was a good idea and to stay positive. Dennis sauntered by as another boy I didn't know ran into school and shoved a slip of paper into his hand. He checked it quickly, then stuffed it in his pocket.

"Okay?" the boy asked Dennis.

"Yeah," Dennis said. "Okay."

Mr. Soboleski, the baseball coach, walked down the hall, and Dennis scooped up an imaginary line drive and threw it hard over his head, causing Mr. Soboleski to slam him on the shoulder shouting, "Dennis, my man!" and the paper to slip silently from Dennis's pocket, which nobody noticed except me. I scooped it up.

"Notes," I explained to Wes. The bell rang, the hall emptied. Wes ran to band, I ran to study hall.

I could do without first-period study hall because it was stupid to take all that trouble to get to school and then do nothing. I covered the paper with my hand and read the short message: "Pool's. Backfarb. 11 P.M."

It did not take a mental giant to figure this out because Cyril Pool lived on Backfarb Road. Cyril *and* Big Daddy. I felt a wave of excitement. Big Daddy was on the hit list. Dennis was the pumpkin thief!

For a few moments I was thrilled. If Big Daddy

was stolen, Max would win. Cyril didn't deserve to win because Cyril was despicable and deeply hated among growers. Pilfering Big Daddy would be the last laugh on a man who had turned the Weigh-In into his own dirty game. By 11:00 P.M. my problems would be over. It was beautifully easy, except for the guilt.

Richard was waiting for me by the giant Thunderbird sculpture Miss Moritz's freshman class had made in honor of the Native American. Richard said it looked like a diseased turkey and Native Americans everywhere should be insulted. A banana peel was thrown over its beak (yesterday there had been an athletic supporter), giving the bird "a rakish appeal," according to Mr. Greenpeace. I clenched the note as Richard and I walked home.

"Well," I said smugly, "you were wrong."

"I doubt it," he said.

"You don't even know what I was going to say."

"It doesn't matter."

"It matters," I insisted, extending the paper. "Read it and weep."

He read it. "So?"

"It was in Dennis's pocket."

"You picked Dennis's pocket?"

"He *dropped* it," I explained as Richard's face darkened. "He's going to hit Cyril's tonight." Richard took this in, examining the note. "It doesn't matter that he bats .340," I said. "He's a lousy thief."

Richard nodded, shocked and angry. "Have you called the police?"

"I'm sort of thinking about it."

Actually, I was thinking about calling them after

11:00 P.M. After Dennis got Big Daddy. After Cyril got what he deserved. After my problems were over.

"You should call them now," said Richard.

"I'm thinking about that, too," I said. Which was partially true. Nana had raised me in the Presbyterian Church with enough guilt to make even petty crime uncomfortable. Nana always said that God sees when others don't and sends the gift of guilt to keep us on the way.

"If you don't," Richard continued, swinging to connect with a speed ball, "it's like being an accessory or worse. It's like"—his face grew menacing—"*throwing the game.*"

"Do you have to bring baseball into everything?"

"Baseball *is* everything," Richard said, taking his ball and glove from his bookbag.

"Look," I shouted, "Dennis is the bad guy here, not me! You've been defending him! You've been—"

"I gave him," Richard interrupted, "the benefit of the doubt."

"You were wrong!"

"That was then," Richard said slowly. "Now I think he should be arrested."

But what, I screamed inside, about *Cyril?* He wouldn't call the police if my name were on that paper. Cyril wouldn't bring a cup of water to a dying gourd that wasn't from his patch. Cyril was going to win and make everyone feel rotten about it and stick it to me for another whole year.

"Winning isn't worth it, Ellie." Richard, God's bringer of guilt, threw his ball dead center into the hole of an oak tree.

"Maybe they could maim his squash a little, just enough to—"

Richard glared at me and retrieved his ball. I knew he was right. He knew he was right and had the backing of the Presbyterian Church. We walked the long way to Cyril's. I saw the sign first: POOL'S PUMPKIN PATCH, HOME OF THE WHOPPER.

"I can't do it," I said to Richard who pushed me forward.

Herman, loyal pumpkin guard, was snoozing by Big Daddy, holding his gun like a teddy bear. Big Daddy gleamed beside him and grew a few more inches just to show he was champ. Richard kicked dirt in Herman's direction who woke up fidgeting, then adjusted his rifle like he was back from a coffee break.

"Where's Cyril?" Richard asked. Herman spat in the direction of the house, a faded yellow frame. We approached the screen door. Cyril's greasy face appeared and broke into a slimy grin.

"Keep comin' back for more, Missy? Somethun' 'bout this place you like, or what?"

During times of trial when character is tested to the limit, I always wanted to be like Nana. Nana could look the biggest lout right in the face and not even shudder. She could tell off a person with such love that person would light a candle for her at church the same day. When the Urices' dog trampled her prize daffodil bed, Nana gave him a cookie, patted him on the head, and told Phil Urice that dogs will be dogs. Phil told the whole town that Nana was next to a saint, which was true, but Nana wasn't here now. I was.

"Cyril," I spat, "you are a conniving, lying, lousy creep, and you don't deserve this act of kindness. I think I can speak for every grower in this area when I—"

Richard was not impressed with my opening, placed his hand on my shoulder, and tugged hard. "I'm only here out of Christian charity," I snarled.

"Which," said Richard, glaring at me, "will start anytime now."

Cyril was used to being insulted and responded by picking his teeth. I sucked in my breath: "All right, Cyril, here it is. We learned that the pumpkin thieves might be coming here tonight. Not that you deserve a warning, but I thought you'd want to know."

Christian charity touched Cyril so deeply that he started laughing—cackling, really—whooping it up like a hyena. "You think, Missy," he gasped, "I'm gonna fall for that?"

I was getting hot now. I had just delivered the toughest line in growing history, ruined my chances of snagging the great Weigh-In blue ribbon, given up regional fame and adulation, and Cyril Pool was laughing at *me!*

"Maybe"—he sneered, stepping out on the porch—"jus' maybe you're the thief, huh? Whatcha say to that?"

"What do I say to that?"

"Cat got yur tongue?"

There are times when words aren't enough. A full watering can was at my feet. I dumped it on Cyril's head. Cyril started blubbering and spitting, which sure made me feel a little better.

"Have a nice day, Cyril," I said.

"Get," he shrieked, "*off my land!*"

"I think he wants us to go," said Richard.

"Yes, indeed."

I stormed off the porch with Richard into the sunset.

The sheriff thanked us for the information and said he'd be there personally when Dennis and his team arrived at Cyril's. Pumpkin thieves were an embarrassment to the sheriff who never knew what to do about them. Maybe Dennis and his band would be hanged at dawn.

Mannie Plummer, who'd lost her two-hundred-pounder, was picketing the station with her seventy-two-year-old sister, waving signs that read: THEY DON'T CARE. THEY REALLY DON'T. The sheriff told Mannie that he cared, he really did, but Mannie started crying and held her sign higher, and what, asked the sheriff, could you do about that? Richard said we were glad to help. Very glad, I added, dying inside, wondering if Cyril could at least be arrested for bad taste.

The night was still. Spider stood guard near the toolshed, hugging a slipper. Max was showing splotchy patches, clear signs of squash stress. Tonight was warmer, but I had my blankets and heater ready to fight off frost. If it wasn't pumpkin thieves, it was something else. You could count on it. The clock moved to midnight and my ears strained for the sound of sirens.

Chapter Eight

Mrs. Lemming ran from door to door with the news the next morning. She was waving her arms all excited because her boy, Spears, the sheriff's deputy, had phoned her at 1:00 A.M. so she could be the first to know.

Actually, Dennis and his rotten cousin were the first to know, being arrested and all, right in the middle of Cyril's patch just before they could chop Big Daddy off his vine at exactly 11:23 P.M. Dennis had put up quite a fight, kicking Spears as he put the handcuffs on and screaming for a lawyer, but Spears was used to foul behavior, being in the service of the law. The sheriff let Spears do most of the work, since the sheriff had a bad back and wasn't too keen on tackling nineteen-year-old thugs. There were three of them, Mrs. Lemming said—Dennis, his cousin, Bart, and a nasty boy from Circleville with tattoos—vicious criminals all of them, with shifty eyes and coal black hearts.

Mrs. Lemming's eyes were wet when she said it was over now—Spears had captured the thieves. Growers could relax and go about their business—Spears was on patrol.

Dennis denied the whole thing. Said he wasn't the pumpkin thief, that he was just passing by Cyril's with a big knife and a pickup at 11:00 P.M., and that the Rock River Sheriff's Department was going to be sorry. Mrs. Lemming called Mannie Plummer and her sister and they went down to glare at Dennis and his band and bring the sheriff and Spears some cranberry strudel, which was Mannie's specialty and which she only doled out at funerals and other special occasions.

I fed Spider some Alpo with a biscuit crumbled on top and wondered why the arrest had to happen before they could cut Big Daddy off the vine. After the fact would have made for a better case, and that's what the law wanted, didn't they?

The sun was warming Max, who stretched to reach the heat. It was good to feel safe again, even though I'd given Cyril the break of his life. I took down my BACK OFF, CREEPS, YOU'RE BEING WATCHED sign and jangled the bells around Max's plot in solemn victory as Spider howled. Ding, dong, the witch is dead. I watered Max, explaining gently that the pumpkin thieves' reign of terror was over. Max's sprinkler system needed adjusting. I set the timer on medium spray for another thirty minutes.

Nana was eating cinnamon buns when I came by, which weren't exactly on my diet, but I didn't want to be rude. I'd gained back a pound since Grace's party and was frustrated with my diet and my life.

"With that glorious news," Nana said, "I thought you'd come sailing in here." I told her I was glad Dennis got caught. "I hear," Nana said, "those boys are in deep trouble."

Yes, I nodded, that was probably true. They deserved it. "And tell me," she said. "How are you?"

"I'm fine."

"You're not either."

"I'm okay then."

Nana nodded and waited. I fidgeted. She said, "It's not over yet, honey. There's ten more days."

"Yes it is, Nana. He's going to win."

Nana wiped her hands and looked at me hard. "Well," she said. "So what if he does?"

So what?

"What if Cyril does win?" she continued. "What does that really mean?"

"It means he wins and sticks it to me."

Nana stomped her foot. "Ellie Morgan," she cried, "I'm ashamed of you, grousing around here like some bad loser. What does it mean if he wins, Ellie? *You tell me*, because I can't seem to get there on my own!"

Nana didn't shout much, but when she did all those times she'd held back came out. "It means," I insisted, "that he was, you know"—she was staring at me so I whispered the last part—"better."

"Better." Nana said the word like she'd missed something. "Better than what?"

"Better," I shouted back, "than *me!*"

"Oh," said Nana, dragging me out back to the porch in full view of her land, "I see." She pointed to her fields that she and Grandpa had sown and harvested and protected and cried over.

"Three years of drought," she said, "two years of infestation. One year the drainage tiles broke and water collected beneath the ground and your grandpa couldn't handle it and it near about finished us. Four years straight the barn needed big fixings, one year of just plain bust. I stopped counting the early frosts and the freezes and the Dutch elm disease that took away all those good, shady trees. All of that, Ellie, over twenty years."

"Nana, I know—"

"You *don't* know," she insisted, "not the way you're acting. Growing's not something you do, it's something you are. It's not a contest, though a little competition makes things interesting. It's always going to be hard, honey, always going to be a challenge. Dealing with nature's like dealing with a slippery pig: You just can't get ahold of it. I could never get that through to your father. He always wanted to be in control."

I looked down at my shoes, which were caked with mud and memories. The air was clear and windless, the sun hit Nana's field like a floodlight. "And," she said, "all this about Cyril sticking it to you is a load of manure, because he can't do anything to you unless you let him, so don't, that's all."

Nana took two fists of earth and put them in my hand. "Things don't matter near as much as your attitude toward them," she said, rubbing some dirt on my cheek, laughing, and sprinkling some on my hair. "Fairy dust," she announced.

I was laughing now, too, tossing dirt in her direction, ducking as she threw some in mine. We were both a mess when it was over. Nana hugged me with her whole self and slapped a hunk of earth in my hand.

"Just in case you forget again," she said.

* * *

I went back home, turned off the sprinklers dousing Max, and checked with a shovel to see how deep the water had gone. More than a foot into the soil: perfect. I washed, changed, and made it to school only fifteen minutes late, not bad considering I had just been rolled in dirt by my grandmother. Justin Julee, the smallest boy in school and prize reporter for the *Rock River High School Defender*, was waiting for me after study hall.

"I want to interview you for the school paper," he announced.

"You're kidding."

"I want," Justin continued, enthusiasm bubbling from him because more than anything in his life he loved reporting, "to capture your thoughts about growing pumpkins and what it's like to have accomplished so much already in this area while still in high school."

"You're kidding."

"The deadline is Thursday," he said. "We need photographs and an interview. You'll be the lead story in our Harvest Festival edition. Okay, Ellie?"

"You're kidding."

He wasn't.

I was an unusual choice for the *Defender* because I wasn't a cheerleader, sports star, or brain. I figured if I totally starved myself I could drop five pounds by Thursday's photo session, but if I ate nothing, I'd probably die and Cyril would dance on my grave. I went for broke and threw away my lunch (meatloaf sandwich on a croissant, a perfect pear, and julienned red peppers) in favor of diet Sprite and a winning smile.

School was full of news about Dennis. One report said that he and his band had been taken to the slammer in Des Moines and forced to share a cell with mass murderers and investment bankers. Another was certain that Dennis's bail had been set for one million dollars and his father wasn't even trying to raise it. Mrs. Lemming's rotten grandson Ralphie said the sheriff and Mannie Plummer had buried Dennis and his cousin alive. Richard stayed quiet, and Mr. Soboleski began looking for a new first baseman.

Ralphie was getting a big kick out of the arrest and suggested loudly in the cafeteria that Dennis's house should at least get T.P.'d and that he, Ralphie, was just the guy to do it. Miss Moritz dragged him to the principal's office, threatening him with additional history assignments if he did *"anything* with toilet paper other than what was originally intended."

A peace came over pumpkin growers near and far as word of the arrest spread through the area. Renée Burgess, director of the Rock River Pedal Pushers, a senior citizens' bicycle club, led seven of her cyclists around Town Hall (slowly because they were old geezers) in "a great lap for freedom and victory." Cyril was interviewed by the *Rock River Clarion* and had his picture on the front page with the sheriff, Spears, and Mrs. McKenna, who declared all pumpkins in the area were now totally liberated.

I sat in the mud with Max and Spider, wondering why the joy of liberation had not reached my heart. I was going to come in second. The silver medal. Second at sixteen years of age, out of hundreds of other growers. That was not bad. That was very, very good. I was going to be interviewed for the lead article in the school paper and be famous. I felt awful and started to cry. An old green truck pulled up, Spider flashed his fangs, and out jumped Wes.

I stopped breathing.

He was wearing brown corduroys and a gold cotton sweater and he looked just great except for his nose, which was red from the cold he'd had. Grace said he'd had a temperature of 102 and was mostly reading and watching TV and unable to visit The Other One in Gaithersville over the weekend. Ha-ha.

"Hi," he said.

"Hi." I sniffed, wiping tears.

"I came at a bad time, huh?"

"No, no, no, no, no . . . I'm okay . . . I'm just—"

"Crying."

"Right."

He sat down with me in the mud and gazed upon Max. His face got far away, then he started grinning like he'd seen a rainbow. "He's incredible," he said, touching Max's hard flesh. Max, always the showoff, seemed to stretch in the sun.

"Thanks."

"You've done something great here, Ellie," said Wes, stroking Max's huge vine. "Can't do this with corn."

How true.

"Why are you crying?" he asked.

I pulled myself together. "I'm not crying any-more."

"Why *were* you crying?" He was giving Max gentle taps across his top and examining his leaves like he had a microscope. What was he going to do next? Kick the tires?

"It's a long story."

"I like stories."

"It's a sad story."

Wes nodded and shook Max's vine. "About how many pounds a day is he growing now?"

101

"Is this an inspection?" I asked.

"Yes," Wes said, on his knees now, checking Max's underbelly. "How many pounds?"

"Uh . . . maybe thirty-six in the past four days . . . it's hard to say."

Wes whistled and jiggled Max, his ear close to Max's skin. "Solid," Wes announced.

"Of course he's solid."

Wes turned to me and brushed the dirt from his pants. "I think you can win, Ellie."

I sighed, deep and sad. I didn't want to talk about Cyril and Big Daddy, who would devour Max in one humongous gulp. I shook my head and sank in the dust.

"I was there," Wes insisted. "Right before I came here. I saw him." He raised his hands like a terrible giant and laughed. *"Big Daddy."*

"You went to see him?" I was numb.

"Yeah, I did."

"Cyril didn't run you off his land with a blow-torch?"

"Nope."

"What were you doing over there? I mean—"

"Spying," Wes said, and laughed his laugh that started in his stomach and worked its way up. "I told him I was president of the Gaithersville Ag Club, which is true because they haven't replaced me yet, and that I'd been hearing about him for years, which isn't exactly true, and that I'd been wanting to shake his hand, which was a downright lie."

"You *touched* Cyril?"

"Only for the cause," Wes said, and looked at Max. I looked at Max, too, because if I looked at Wes I'd turn red, not a sophisticated move. "Then I told him I'd heard about his pumpkin and could I possibly see it and tell all the kids back in Gaithersville? You know."

"You *said* that?"

"Pretty much, yeah. I wanted to see what you were up against."

I sat quietly, my heart thumping. I was in love. Wes had gone to see the competition for *me*? "But Cyril's going to beat me by at least a hundred pounds," I explained. "You saw it! I can't catch up. That thing is enormous, it's unbeatable, it's perfect, it's—"

"Rotting," Wes said.

"What?"

"Rotting, Ellie. I swear. It's just started so I could hardly tell, but once my aunt Izzy's prize pumpkin started to go before its time, so I've seen this before."

"Rotting," I said.

"*And* ripe." Wes was grinning. "Big Daddy's ripe already, the vine's withering, the stem's dry. The skin's softening just a bit under the belly. I don't know how it happened, but—"

Rotting. The thought was too wonderful to be true.

"He could make it to the Weigh-In, maybe," Wes continued, "but he's not going to get any bigger. And if that rot starts really spreading . . ."

Please, God, let it spread.

"He's soup. Either way," Wes said, "Cyril's going to have to cut him off the vine in the next couple of days, which gives you ten days to catch up at ten pounds a day. . . ."

I looked at Max, who suddenly became Super Squash right there. I rose from the dust. "All right," I said, brushing myself off. "We're going for it."

"Good," said Wes. I stood there, not sure what was next. "What are you going to do?" he asked.

"I thought I'd start by standing."

Wes shook his head. "You've got to talk to him, Ellie."

"*I talk to him!*"

"Show me," Wes insisted.

Show him? You don't talk to a pumpkin in the presence of someone you want more than anything in the world to like you. Any loyal reader of *Seventeen* knows that!

"I can't," I said shyly, "it's . . . you know . . ."

Wes scowled, grabbed my hand, and put it on Max's vine. "Don't get soft on me now," he said. "I hate girls who go soft."

I thought boys liked girls like Sharrell who were soft through and through and couldn't open bottletops or fix electronic sprinklers.

"You've got to get tough now," Wes insisted.

Get tough? Give me a break. I mashed a beetle and bared my teeth. Wes knelt in the dirt and put both hands on Max. He closed his eyes like he was praying, but I didn't think he was. "Max," he said gently, "you are the greatest squash I've ever seen, greater even than my aunt Izzy's, and I thought I'd never say that." Breathless, I patted Max to let him know that was true as Wes continued. "Max, you've probably felt another pumpkin in the area, one who you think might be a little bigger than you?" Max shuddered at this. "He's rotting, Max. Through and through. And you're going to take his place. You're filling with hope now—hope that you can do it. I want you," directed Wes, "to gain eleven pounds a day starting now."

Wes stroked Max's skin right there in broad daylight. He massaged his vine and patted his leaves. "That's good, Max," he said. "That's good." Wes sat back satisfied and turned to me. "That's how you've got to do it."

I sat next to Wes, not too close, you understand, but close enough to make the point. I wanted him to know I was tough, but that I needed some help in this talking business with pumpkins that he was obviously great at, being a sensitive grower and all. I wanted him to know that what he had just done was the most wonderful thing I had ever seen in the whole world and I would never forget it.

"I need help," I croaked. Wes looked at me. "And that doesn't mean I'm soft, okay?"

Wes took my hand and squeezed it. My hand was sweating pretty bad and I needed to wipe it off, but that didn't seem like a great idea, given the fact it was being used.

"I'll help you," he said.

My heart stopped beating, but I was still alive.

"Okay," I said, squeezing his hand back. "But only if you have time. You don't have to go out of your way or anything."

Chapter Nine

It was **Thursday.** Eight days to go.

I was hoarse from all the sensitive pumpkin talking I was directing at Max. There's just so much you can say to a squash, and I was getting desperate for new material. I played Dad's tape *You and You Alone* for Max in a moment of weakness and suggested he "look forward to each new day with anticipation and love for all humanity."

I tried the direct approach: I slapped Max's vine and told him to push past his fear of success, be a man, and go for gargantuan. I, after all, had lost three pounds already this week and was going for size ten, an equally distant goal.

Wes had been by yesterday and brought pictures of giant pumpkins from his aunt Izzy's World Pumpkin Federation newsletter. Huge ones—650 to 690 pounds—from England, Australia, and France. He showed them to Max: "This," Wes directed softly, "is what a pumpkin was meant to do, Max." Wes and I stood quietly together until his sneezing jag killed the mood. He blew his nose, and reached out to take my hand when Richard appeared, blabbering about the Chicago Cubs and the strength of the National League. I glared at Richard, Wes glared at Richard. Richard, oblivious, grinned and oiled his glove.

"Well," said Richard after Wes left, "that was nice."

"Did it ever occur to you that we wanted to be alone?"

Richard looked around. "We *are* alone."

I stamped my foot. "I *meant* Wes and me! Could you possibly consider that?"

Richard considered it. "What's for dinner?" he asked.

"Chicken breast and broccoli."

"With skin or without?"

"Without. Skin is bad for you."

"Potatoes?" he asked hopefully. "Rice?"

"Nothing," I sneered. "Dry, lifeless, lo-cal."

"You could die from that."

"I'm going to be gorgeous," I reminded him, sucking in my stomach.

"It's no way to live," he said, and slumped home to have frozen dinners with his mother.

Already Max had beaten every previous record from the Rock River Pumpkin Weigh-In and Harvest Fair. He was bigger than anything, except for Big Daddy, who was still on the vine, still sucking up Cyril's good soil—and hopefully rotting his brains out. Any caring grower would have cut Big Daddy off the vine and let him cure in the sun to dry the stem and stop bacteria and mold from spreading. But Cyril didn't care if his squash was sick and needed medical attention. As long as Big Daddy stayed on the vine, he might suck up a few extra pounds. As long as Big Daddy could hold together and get on the scale in eight days, Cyril would win and he knew it.

Richard was watching Cyril's moves from behind the barn on the old Winger property. Cyril, he said, was under pressure, and Herman wasn't spitting with the same spunk.

"He comes out and shakes the vine," Richard said, "sticks his ear on the skin to listen. Then he looks real worried and goes away."

"That's good," I said. "How's it look to you?"

"Still too early to call." Richard blew a giant bubble with his gum and peered at me from behind it.

"You could lie to me. You could tell me to be encouraged, that good will triumph over evil."

"Good will triumph over evil," said Richard.

"Liar."

Justin Julee and I sat in the back of Miss Moritz's empty classroom that had been decorated with World War II battle maps and posters of popular war sayings like "The slip of a lip can sink a ship." Gina Carlucci's grandmother had baked cannolis for the class to remind us that there was more to Italy than Palermo and Sicily. My cannoli was sitting in my stomach like a lead pipe, pushing against my khaki slacks, which I was wearing along with my floppy orange blouse and Mother's earrings that made me look deeply sophisticated. Justin asked me how I protected Max from pumpkin thieves and I told him about Spider and the bells and my natural ability to sense doom. Justin wrote as I talked about the extreme pressures of champion squash competition and how you had to be strong to fight off all the terror Mother Nature threw your way.

I told him that some of the bravest people on earth grew giant pumpkins, which he hadn't realized, and I said most people didn't. Kids stopped and looked in the room as we talked, which made me toss my head to make Mother's earrings dance. I decided I could really get used to fame.

Mrs. Lemming's grandson Ralphie was the school photographer. Photography was the only thing he was any good at; even Mrs. Lemming said so. Ralphie was checking the light and snapping candid shots from my good side and announced that it was time to take a picture of me and Max together.

We piled into Ralphie's red pickup that had leather seats and a wooden steering wheel. He bought it after selling his prize photograph of baby pigs at sundown to *Life* magazine. Nana said the photograph, which hung for months near the overdue book desk in the Rock River Library, was sensitive, funny, and caring. I mentioned to her that Ralphie was none of those things, and how could he turn out such wonderful work? Nana said life wasn't fair and just to get used to it.

Spider heard Ralphie's truck and started shrieking. Ralphie threw him a hunk of beef jerky, which quieted him right down. Justin stood silently before Max like he was at a shrine.

"You did *this*," whispered Justin, dwarfed by Max's shadow.

"It was nothing," I offered humbly.

Ralphie got some good shots of me and Max, including some action sequences where I chased away a crow, which, Justin said, gave the feeling of the constant battle of the patch. Justin said it was one of the most interesting interviews he'd ever done and that he was going home to write it up tonight, he was so excited. Even Ralphie seemed impressed with Max and gave Spider another piece of beef jerky and scratched his neck in friendship.

"One more thing, Ellie," said Justin, "for the record. Do you think you're going to win?"

Now, this was a trick question. If I said yes and lost, I'd look like a jerk and be on the record, and if I said no I'd lose my competitive edge, not to mention my newly found fame, which I was getting real used to. So I said what Mr. Soboleski always said before a big game he wasn't sure his team could pull off. "We're going to go out there and do what we have to do," I said, and looked off into the sunset. Justin nodded solemnly, Ralphie gunned his motor and screeched away in a cloud of dust.

The latest from Spears was that Dennis hotly denied he was the pumpkin thief, despite being caught red-handed. Dennis's cousin swore this was the first time they'd tried to steal a vegetable and they didn't want to get blamed for all the others the sheriff was trying to pin on them, going back to World War II, when, Dennis insisted, he wasn't even alive yet, and even if he was, he couldn't drive. Spears told Mrs. Lemming that the sheriff slapped ten other indictments on the boys and was whistling around the station doing little jigs with his bad back. Now he could go into town with his head high and not get the Bronx cheer blasted at him from Mannie Plummer's sister, who sat on the porch of Kay's Koffee Kup, his favorite snack shop, when she wasn't picketing the station. Mannie Plummer said she recognized Dennis's truck as *the* truck that pulled away from her house under fire on that tragic, fateful morning. Ed Meegan said he'd seen Dennis's cousin in Circleville trying to sell a huge squash to a funeral director. Mr. Soboleski wondered if Dennis could be paroled by spring in time for the opening game.

Wes met me outside Miss Moritz's class. He was carrying his clarinet case and bad news. Worse even than the news I was about to give Miss Moritz regarding my midsemester paper, "What I Would Do Differently If I Were General Patton," due today, which I had not started. Given General Patton's personality, this could take all year.

Grace McKenna, a pacifist, could not relate to war and had written only two paragraphs. She said Patton did pretty well under the circumstances with all that shooting and Field Marshal Montgomery getting all that press. She said we should all try to get along and then there would be no more wars. The one thing she would have changed was Patton's famous weather prayer. Grace didn't feel battle should be easy and that demanding a prayer be written by the chaplain for good weather was unsportsmanlike conduct. God, Grace said, sends the weather *He* wants, and it is our responsibility to accept it.

Wes put his hand on my shoulder glumly and delivered his news. "Freezing rain," he announced, "turning to hail. Expected this weekend."

"I'm finished," I said.

"Not necessarily," Wes answered. "We can cover him with a hundred blankets and—"

"Cyril's squash will freeze," I said, which he knew already, "which will preserve it till the Weigh-In. Max will stop growing. I'm dead."

Wes looked at me hard: "You have to keep trying, Ellie."

"I'm too tired."

I slumped against the wall. The bell had rung and I hadn't noticed. Miss Moritz asked Wes if he would like to join the class or go to his scheduled period, which made most of the class snicker and me turn red and Wes run off to Spanish with Señor "Ted" Morales. I crawled into my seat as Miss Moritz walked from desk to desk collecting midsemester Patton papers.

"Well?" she said, poised before me.

"It's almost done," I lied.

She regarded me coldly. "*Almost* doesn't count."

Tell me about it. You could kill yourself for an entire season, grow the greatest pumpkin of your whole life, and get blasted out of the box by hail, freezing rain, and a brain-dead sludge. If I were General Patton I would have had a million weather prayers commissioned by as many chaplains as I could find just in case God was feeling patriotic.

Richard and his mother, my aunt Peg, were staying overnight because their water heater broke and flooded their basement. Richard had cleaned most of it up but Wallace, the repairman, couldn't make it until Saturday afternoon, and the prospect of a damp house with no hot water did not thrill Aunt Peg. She was getting around pretty well with her crutches now, most of the pain was gone from her face, and she was laughing and carrying on just like she used to before the accident.

Aunt Peg was a beautiful woman with dark brown hair and aqua eyes, the kind of woman that men always looked at and wanted to be around. Aunt Peg was not good at picking men and had given them up on several occasions, having had a rotten marriage to Richard's father (my mother's brother, Ken), who was a handsome gambler and a world-class chump. She had a three-week engagement to Spears, who, she said, was a fine assistant deputy and who should probably just concentrate on that. Aunt Peg believed in being kind and that the words we speak on earth will follow us wherever we go. Everyone knew that Spears was still in love with Aunt Peg. Nana said men named Ken were always trouble.

I made pot roast with tomato ginger gravy, mashed potatoes, tossed salad with mustard vinaigrette, and brown sugar apple cake. Nana came for dinner, too, and said it was the best pot roast she had ever tasted. Richard had thirds and Aunt Peg said I'd make a wonderful wife someday but to watch all men carefully because they could turn on a dime. It was a fine evening surrounded by my family. Everyone clucked over Max except Dad. It was just what Max and I needed, because tomorrow the hail was coming.

A few cowardly growers like Gloria Shack were cutting their pumpkins off the vine tonight, even though it was still reasonably warm, and bringing them inside for safety before the hail hit. Wes had dropped off nine blankets for Max and was coming over tomorrow with more. Nana, Richard, and I played Scrabble against Dad and Aunt Peg as Max braced himself for the worst. It was Friday night, and nobody wanted to go to sleep. We played until well past midnight and ate the entire brown sugar apple cake and two bags of barbecued potato chips.

I was about to get a triple word score for "freezing" *with* a triple letter on the "z," which would cinch my team's win and destroy Dad's earlier score with "quagmire" when Spider shrieked. Spider shrieking was nothing new, but this was a shriek followed by nothing, which didn't figure, because Spider always shrieked in triplicate. I got up, and Richard pushed me down. Richard had finally found a place for "macho" on a double word with a double letter on the "c" and wasn't feeling patient. "Freezing" was possibly one of the great Scrabble moves of all time, and I shoved it in Dad's face as Aunt Peg groaned in bitter defeat.

Then I heard the sound. I dismissed it at first because Spider didn't respond, but it was a low-pitched hum, like the chugging of an engine. I heard it again and went to the back window. Spider lay on the ground licking something, probably a smelly old slipper. Max sat sturdily in his patch. The noise had stopped. Strange. Richard was playing "macho" with great fanfare when I saw it. It was big and reddish and pushed by three hooded figures. It didn't register at first what was really happening, but then everything came into focus as I watched the truck back into *my* patch and inch toward *my* squash!

Pumpkin thieves!

I screamed for Dad and Richard, grabbed a rolling pin, and pushed out the door. A ski-masked figure stood over Max with a huge knife, ready to cut his vine. I lunged toward him, screeching. He turned, shocked, and dropped his knife, but that wasn't good enough.

Max's automatic sprinkling system controls were at my feet. I cranked the dial to high and let the lashing water nail him good. He covered his face as the hard water hit and I raced toward him shaking my rolling pin, screaming like a soldier gunning down the enemy.

The rotten thieves were shouting to each other to get moving, get out of here, when the cavalry came on the scene. Dad tore past me, running after two of them. The driver went for the truck but was stopped short by a perfectly thrown baseball hitting him square on the shoulder. He fell to the ground as his buddies ran for the street, but they were no match for Dad. His long legs made up speed as the villains tripped over my compost mixture bags trying to escape. Dad grabbed one by the hood and hit another with a bag of pearlite and threw them on the ground. I shoved a hose at the drenched robber and caught him in the face.

"If you move," I shouted, holding the rolling pin over him as Richard ran up beside me with his bat. I couldn't think of anything more scary to say, so I glared at him with hate. Streams of water crashed around us, but I stayed tough. Spider was barking furiously now, finally getting the point.

"Bad man, Spider!" I shouted, pointing at Max's enemy. Nana turned off the sprinkler and charged through the patch, shaking my best sauté pan over her head, shouting the law was coming and if anybody moved, she'd bang him good. Dad stood over his prisoners and didn't have to say anything because he was 6'6". Aunt Peg hobbled on the porch with her crutches and said Spears was on the way like it was the worst news of her life.

"Are you all right, Ellie?" Dad shouted.

"I'm okay, Dad."

Richard told our prisoner that in Rock River they burned pumpkin thieves at the stake in the middle of town in broad daylight. I wiped the water from my face as my enemy shook with terror.

"You," I spat, "are a rotten, moldy creep!" The thief sighed. I glared at Spider. "This," I asked, "is the pumpkin thieves' worst nightmare?"

Spider licked the thief's hand. "I think you tamed him, Ellie," Richard said. "See. You are a dog person."

A siren ricocheted from the north up Bud DeWitt Memorial Drive, growing louder as Spider shrieked his warning. "Thank you, Spider," I spat. "But I think they're on our side." Spears and the sheriff marched across the yard, guns ready. Spears grinned and waved at Aunt Peg, who hobbled quickly away.

"Take your ski mask off, son," the sheriff directed my robber, but he didn't move. "Off!" ordered the sheriff.

Slowly the robber stood on his feet. His hands pulled the mask to his nose. Then he threw it off and stared at the ground.

Nana said, "Oh, my."

Richard said he couldn't believe it and dropped his bat.

Spears gasped.

The sheriff shook his head sadly and pulled out his handcuffs.

Aunt Peg said she might take a nice walk around the neighborhood.

I looked at my enemy cold in the face and I guess I should have figured.

There in the mud and the slop stood Mrs. Lemming's rotten grandson Ralphie! Ralphie, who had heard all my secrets, checked out my property, befriended my dog, taken pictures of my good side! Ralphie turned to his uncle Spears and said, "Look, it's not what you think." Spider, noble guard dog, wagged his tail and pulled a bag of beef jerky from Ralphie's wet pocket unashamed. Aunt Peg hobbled upstairs and locked herself in the guest room. Max seemed to shiver as a cold, wet wind blew in from the east.

Chapter
Ten

It was up for grabs as to which band had stolen more pumpkins, Dennis's or Ralphie's. No one was making any predictions, and Spears was staying quiet. Arresting a nephew wasn't an experience every lawman gets to have, and Spears was taking it real hard, but not as hard as Mrs. Lemming, who had drawn her chintz curtains in disgrace and refused to come out of her house. Mannie Plummer said it was a dark day for the Lemming family and left a cranberry strudel on Mrs. Lemming's screened-in porch so she'd know no one blamed her and so the sneaky raccoon that drove Mrs. Lemming crazy couldn't get at it either.

Penny Penstrom, the sheriff's secretary/dispatcher, called Nana to say that for the first time in history the jail was full. Spears, she said, couldn't take Ralphie's mournful wails, and the sheriff felt that eight robbers in two cells was pushing Fate. Ralphie's father showed up at 3:00 A.M., paid his bail, and dragged Ralphie home by his nose hairs. Ralphie's mother would have come, but she collapsed in the driveway from shame and was helped to the couch by her only good son, Butchie. Three other robbers, all age eighteen, were moved to Circleville. Dennis's father told the sheriff to keep him. Penny said *this* was a story that would make Rock River proud and that my incredible cool under pressure should be recognized. Dennis, she reported, was blaming all squash stealing on Ralphie, who was blaming all squash stealing on Dennis. The sheriff was treating himself to a two-hour breakfast at Kay's Koffee Kup and thinking about running for mayor.

I had been up all night guarding Max, except for two hours when Richard wrapped himself in a blanket and sat in the patch with his bat. Richard was sleeping on the living-room couch, and I was fixing cornbread and Canadian bacon when Gordon Mott, publisher of the *Rock River Clarion*, an extremely important, big-deal newspaper, stuck his head in my kitchen and said, "You're hot news, kid. Did you know that?"

I was about as shocked as a person could be but I pulled myself together, said, "Of course I know that," flipped a piece of Canadian bacon, and missed the griddle.

Dad came down, and he and Gordon Mott sat on the back porch. Soon, Gordon Mott said, the whole state would know about me and Max and Ralphie's despicable trick because mine was the kind of news story that people ate up. Gordon Mott knew these things because he used to be the managing editor of the *Chicago Tribune* before he had a beard and before he took early retirement at forty-six "due to five peptic ulcers and cringing, riveting anxiety." He bought the *Rock River Clarion* two years ago and promised to keep his eyes on world events but to print only news that was non-ulcer-producing.

"Your story's got everything, kid," he told me, shoving his photographer in Max's direction. "Action, courage, love, death—"

"No one's died, sir—"

"Death comes in many forms, kid. Trust me on this."

Gordon Mott was rich and carefree, having done very well indeed in the stock market during what he called his "Chicago period," when people called him "Gordo." He now lived on the scenic banks of the Rock River in a fifteen-room house with his third wife, Laura, who was someday going to bake the world's largest pumpkin pie and cinch the title in the *Guinness Book of World Records*. His only daughter, Marsha, collected puréed pumpkin for her mother, got straight A's, and really missed Chicago.

"Okay, kid," said Gordon Mott, positioning me behind Max and walking back and forth like a great guru seeking the meaning of life. "Tell me what happened last night."

"We were playing Scrabble—"

Gordon Mott scrunched up his face and shook his head. "From the heart, kid. From the heart." I told him from the heart. The agony, the terror, the desperation, the sprinkler.

"Nice touch with the sprinkler," Gordon Mott offered. "Makes a great close." He was glowing in the sunshine, a tough man who'd found a tender story. The photographer motioned me against the backdrop of the gathering storm clouds and told me to look into the wind.

"It gets me right here," Gordon Mott said, indicating his stomach. I nodded. Dad nodded. It got us there, too. He circled Max, his face lost in headlines. "It's a story of America at its best," he cried. "Tough and unrelenting—triumphant against the odds—a family pulling together." He slapped his stomach: "That's what sells papers. Those poor slobs in Chicago think all people want is bad news. I spent seventeen years behind a news desk. What'd I get? Inner peace? World vision? I got wars, famine, and heartbreak. I got ulcers enough to count. Bad news gives you ulcers. Trust me on this, kid."

Mr. Mott said he was going to write a story such as the world had never seen and that when he got through, Rock River would be on the map and I would have put it there. "No pressure, kid, but what're your chances of snagging this Weigh-In?" I told him about Cyril and Big Daddy. "If you've got any miracles to work on the vegetable," he said, "I'd start now. Everybody loves a winner. America doesn't do second place unless it's absolutely unavoidable." Then Gordon Mott climbed into his silver BMW and sped off in a cloud of dust.

I sat with Max in the field, considering our newfound fame. "We're a hit, Max," I said. "You think Cyril and Big Daddy could win the heart of the entire state? Not a chance, Max. They haven't got it"—I patted my stomach—"here, where it counts. Trust me on this."

Dad brought a plate of Canadian bacon and cornbread out to the patch on a tray like it was room service. "Well." He beamed, smiling at Max.

He'd never smiled at Max before, and this was a grin so big it made me nervous. "What's wrong?" I asked.

Old Abe patted Max's vine and said, "That's a fine vegetable you have there, Ellie."

I said, *"Huh?"* as Old Abe, cool and pressed, now sat in the dirt like a regular guy. "You're sitting in the dirt, Dad."

"Yes, dear, I know."

"You hate dirt."

Dad smiled, ate a circle of bacon, and handed me one. "I think," said Dad, "I've been very wrong about things." I was quiet because Dad was never wrong, according to him. "It occurred to me," Dad said, "that what you've done with Max here is most astonishing and everyone seems to know it except me."

I checked Dad's pupils. They were normal. He ran his fingers through the dirt like he was touching it for the first time. Spider chased a woodchuck behind the shed and gave up when he found an old slipper.

"My father," Dad continued, "insisted I love farming. I couldn't do it. Our relationship never survived. He told me I'd never leave Iowa. I told him he was dead wrong. I'd leave as soon as I could and only come back for Christmas dinner. He said I'd find the place in me where farming was supposed to be and let it grow." Dad looked at the back porch for a long time. "It's too late to tell him he was half right."

Dad sat deeper in the dirt, and a quiet broke over his face that I hadn't seen in years. "Watching you last night, Ellie, seeing the interest people have in what you've done, I seem to have found it."

"I'm not sure what you're saying."

"I'm saying," Dad explained, "that I've found farming again."

My father? A farmer?

"You start sneezing when you get near Nana's barn," I reminded him.

"That's true."

"You eat sushi."

"I do."

"You're going to take Japanese lessons; you watch foreign films—"

"With subtitles," Dad offered.

"Subtitles." I winced. "Your fingernails are always clean." I checked mine—grungy—and sat on my hands. "That's a dead giveaway, you know, and what about that silk sport jacket from Chicago? You sleep late. You *can't* be a farmer!"

"You're absolutely right," Dad said, standing and brushing off his trousers. "I can't. But I'm going to help you be one, if that's what you want for yourself." Dad paused like he did on his tapes for a hard truth to sink in. I ate two pieces of cornbread without chewing. "It occurred to me, Ellie, that in fighting you I was fighting myself. Your grandmother's been trying to get that through to me for years. This morning it finally sunk in." He extended his hand. "I'm sorry, honey."

I looked at his hand—it was manicured and smooth. I wiped the dirt off mine and shook Dad's hand quickly. I cleared my throat; Dad harrumphed. I patted compost mixture around Max's base to ground him for the storm and threw some dirt at a woodchuck who was getting on my nerves. Dad hugged me hard and told me he was sorry again. I hugged him back and got dirt all over his shirt.

"I can help you," Dad said, "gain a new perspective with Max here." I didn't need a new perspective. I needed a tornado to hit Cyril's patch.

"Winning," Dad said softly, "is my specialty. I think I can help you win." I sighed because when Dad applied himself it always came with emotional perspiration.

"Stand up," he directed. "Repeat after me—"

"I'm a little beat, Dad, could we do this—"

"Stand!" I stood. "Now repeat after me: I reject all past negative programming."

I whispered it: "I reject all past negative programming."

"I believe in myself and the gift within me."

"I believe in myself," I said, "and the gift within me."

"Nothing will hold me back," Dad ordered. "Not weather, not fear, not discouragement. I am called to *this* task at *this* time." I said it, sensing courage. "My father," said Dad, "is not going to fight me anymore. He promises." I said that, too, as two woodchucks snuck up behind Max, their knives and forks ready. Dad stamped his mighty foot and banished them from the patch.

The hail came after lunch just like "The Early-Morning Farm Report" predicted. Richard had left with his mother to wait for Warren the repairman. Wes arrived dressed for battle in a heavy parka with gloves and lugging seven more blankets. We covered Max with two reemay cloths and sixteen blankets to absorb shock, dug a runoff ditch, and lined the ground under his belly with drainage tiles. Wes told me to picture being on a warm beach with Max at my side sucking up sunshine and vitamin C. Storm clouds gathered like dark invaders ready to strike.

Wes rubbed Max's stem and told him to hold on. Wes was still sniffling from his stubborn cold and about to be pelted with hailstones. I wanted him to know I thought he was the most wonderful boy I'd ever met and when this was over we would be a solid couple. This concept was tough to introduce, since we always talked about Max, growing, and his aunt Izzy, who sounded like a motivational squash therapist: "She could stand in front of a pumpkin that was withering, Ellie, I mean *withering* on the vine, look it straight in the eye, and tell it it looked fine."

The rain fell cold and fast. The clouds poured down, the sky went black, the wind whooshed stronger. "Here we go!" Wes cried as we held down the blankets covering Max. Puddles were appearing, the cold mud sloshing against our boots.

"Hang on!" he shouted, pulling a blanket back in place. "I can see it now. Eighty-five degrees, southern Florida, watermelon, lemonade, the surf."

"You're certifiable!"

"Max," Wes roared, "don't listen to her! It's warm, Max! Warm and toasty! Can you feel it?"

Max seemed to dig his heels in as the rain turned to slush and then to hail. Hanging out in a hailstorm, many say, is not intelligent or fun. They're right. The hail came down in small stones at first, but soon the black clouds pushed together and squeezed out giant balls that hit ferociously. We buried our noses in the blankets to cover our faces and hung tight to Max. Dad ran outside in his thigh-high fishing boots, holding a huge tarp. He flung it over us and ducked underneath. "Well," Dad said from under the tarp's darkness, "you must be Wes."

"Yes, sir."

The tarp was a brilliant move, shielding us from the cold wind and the sting of the hailstones' landing. We held it high like a tent over Max.

"When this is over," Dad continued, "I'd like to shake your hand, Wes."

Wes said that would be fine and sneezed. The hail kept coming, but we stood fast, protecting Max from devastation. Ice balls collected on the ground. We sang "Ninety-nine Bottles of Beer on the Wall" three times, "Old Man River," and hummed the "Michigan Fight Song."

But I didn't think we could make it. What was I trying to prove? I looked at Wes. His look back to me said it all. I steadied myself as the hail slowed like the last kernels of popcorn left in a hot pan.

"Is it over?" Dad asked.

Wes peered out and gasped. He threw off the tarp to reveal a land of frozen ice balls sculptured on fences, roofs, and trees. Wes kicked hailstones from Max's base. Dad went for the shovel and cleared a two-foot circular path around the patch.

"There," said Dad, patting Max. "I don't see how Cyril Pool could have possibly survived that."

We had beaten the odds and had a fine celebration of hot cider, grilled cheese and bacon sandwiches with honey mustard, and pears. It was wonderful cooking for Wes, and he even helped me heat the cider. Twice our shoulders touched at the stove, and he smiled at me during both of his coughing fits.

We drank a toast to Big Daddy's demise and didn't say anything nasty about Cyril until the end. The sun was shining nicely, the ice was melting nicely, and the five-day forecast through Thursday on "The Early-Morning Farm Report" was good weather with gentle wind. Perfect for drying out soggy ground. Perfect for plugging in electric blankets and warming squashes. Perfect for the Rock River Pumpkin Weigh-In and Harvest Fair's opening day. Nana called and I told her everything was perfect.

Richard, just returned from the old Winger property on his regular weekend spying mission, called to break the balloon. Cyril and Herman had rigged a shack of two-by-fours with a plywood roof over Big Daddy to protect him from hail, natural disasters, and nuclear war.

"You mean," I shouted, "Big Daddy survived? The hail, the freezing rain—"

"Didn't touch him. Sorry."

"But Cyril doesn't have the brains to think of something like that!"

"Maybe," said Richard, "he hired a consultant."

"Big Daddy's rotting to death," I grumbled. "I know it."

"I guess we'll see," Richard said, "on Thursday."

Chapter Eleven

The *Rock River Clarion* hit Robertson's Newsstand ("All the news that's fit to sell") Sunday morning—Nana was the first in line and bought twenty-two copies and a Baby Ruth. The first installment of Gordon Mott's four-part series about me and Max was front-page center: "Go for It: The Story of a Girl and Her Pumpkin." He called me "a new American heroine with a courageous heart," which was absolutely true, and an "honors student," which was absolutely fiction, guaranteed to make Miss Moritz choke.

Justin, who had been out of town visiting his grandmother, read the article and went into deep, cosmic panic. The *Defender*, he screamed, was coming out to the entire school Monday morning with *no* mention of Ralphie or the arrest. *He* was going to look like a fool. *Why* hadn't he been notified? I told him he wouldn't look like as big a fool as Ralphie who found out too late that heinous crime doesn't pay.

Wes called to congratulate me on being brave and to say he had a 104-degree fever and wouldn't be around for a while. I felt awful and apologized for everything. He said he'd think warm thoughts in Max's direction, sneezed with greatness, and hung up. Mannie Plummer called to say I looked pasty in the *Clarion*'s cover photo and to rub a little rouge on my cheeks the next time. Nana said she'd never been so proud. Dad said I looked extremely motivated and filled with potential. Mrs. McKenna called to say that *this* was the press coverage needed to propel the Rock River Pumpkin Weigh-In and Harvest Fair to world-wide prominence.

Nana had me autograph each newspaper for friends and family. She said that this was going to be a whirlwind week and that true champions always keep perspective. I assured her, while applying double-strength lash-building mascara, that nothing had changed—I was the same humble Ellie. Nana said one tube of mascara per eye was probably enough. JoAnn and Grace came over and we decided the best way to handle fame was to love it. I practiced writing my signature round and bold for autograph seekers as JoAnn and Grace rummaged through my closet for the "right" outfits to wear throughout the week.

I had always wanted to walk down the hall at school and have people notice me like they noticed Sharrell. JoAnn said that even though Sharrell was a head-turner, she'd never made the front page of the *Clarion*. I knew as I walked through the double doors of Rock River High that my entire life had changed. I paused at the drinking fountain, tossed Mother's earrings, and floated to first-period study hall.

Mr. Greenpeace shook my hand, Mr. Soboleski slapped my shoulder, Miss Moritz clucked her tongue and said that *"honors students* are never late turning in midterm papers on General Patton." Crash Bartwald, Rock River's ace quarterback who had never so much as looked in my direction, asked if Max and I would ride in a float for the Homecoming Parade. Justin Julee slapped the *Defender* on my desk with a photocopied "late-breaking news addition" taped under my story. Justin said it made the edition look aesthetically lousy and amateurish, but at least Rock River High would have the hard news he had promised to deliver when he took his journalistic oath. He'd been up all night taping them on and didn't want to hear any cracks.

I was surrounded by kids in the cafeteria, surrounded by people in the halls—people who had not been my friends before but who were now at my side like old buddies.

Gordon Mott came to school to interview my teachers and classmates for his second "A Girl and Her Pumpkin" article. Miss Moritz described me as "a creative thinker who always brought something to class discussion." God didn't strike her dead. Justin showed Gordon Mott his article and said that the entire school was behind me, and that he, Justin, was in particular, always had been, and would be covering the festival for the *Defender.* Sharrell said we'd been friends for years. Mr. Soboleski said he was sure I was going to win, sure I would do the school proud, and sure that Rock River High would have a bang-up baseball season with Dennis's replacement, the new first baseman, Bart Tiller. Bart Tiller said he was going to go out there and do what he had to do.

Fifty-four kids told me to have a good day when Richard and I left to go home. Richard was used to some of this because after a big game, partial baseball stars often get mobbed.

"I know how you feel," he said. "People are always impressed by the wrong stuff."

I thought about that as we walked to Nana's. Here I was, a great and famous pumpkin personality at age sixteen. The world was at my feet all because of Ralphie, who was hanging by his earlobes in his father's barn, doing deep penance.

"It's strange the way it works," Richard continued. "You don't get famous by being sure and steady. You've got to make the big play. And it doesn't matter if you do it in practice. You've got to do it when people are looking." Richard threw his ball perfectly into a hollow log, like I'd seen him do a hundred times. "So you give the fans what they want, you know?"

"I don't know . . . something about that makes me sad."

"You made it, so enjoy it."

"Commercial endorsements?" I kidded.

"You need an agent first."

"I'm a grower. I don't need an agent."

"An agent," explained Richard, "lines that stuff up and protects you."

"From what?"

Richard thought: "From endorsing a line of frozen pumpkin pies that would give half the country food poisoning and kill your career."

"I can't think about this."

"You wouldn't have to think about it if you had an agent."

Nana was on the phone when we arrived. She was trying to convince Mrs. Lemming to come out of her house, but Mrs. Lemming was frozen in shame and wasn't budging. Nana told Mrs. Lemming that staying inside was bad for the soul and that she should decorate her house (the last on the parade route) for the festival like she always did, because she wasn't to blame for Ralphie's lowdown ways. Nobody, Nana explained, *ever* blamed the grandmother of a boy who went bad. It was *always* the parents' fault, so she could hold her head high.

I loved the days before the festival. It was better than Christmas. Wooden pumpkins sprang up on lawns and porches. Pumpkins of every size filled wheelbarrows and baskets near doorways and store windows. Blinking lights and harvest scenes framed Marion Avenue's retail row. Phil Urice dressed like a pumpkin and walked the streets shouting, "Ho, ho, ho!" Even the streetlights were painted orange and repainted gray again in time for election day.

Rock River's three hotels filled with returning family and old friends who'd come back to the scenic shores to clomp across Marion Avenue and sniff the smell of pumpkin in the air once again. Hotels within twenty-five miles bulged with visitors. The event had grown to almost the size of a small state fair, and accounted for 89 percent of the town's yearly profit. It had produced one star, Freddy Bass—three-time winner of the festival's statewide oratory contest, now a television sports commentator for the second-place ABC affiliate in Boise.

Frieda Johnson sold cemetery decorations of orange and brown dyed carnations. Rock River's dead population stayed in style throughout the year thanks to Frieda, but never did the gravestones explode with such gaiety as during festival days. Mr. Soboleski erected a five-foot wooden pumpkin by his dear mother's grave across from Mannie Plummer's father's plot. Mannie complained the Soboleski pumpkin was in bad taste and blocked her father's view of Founders' Square below. Mr. Soboleski moved it one foot back, trimmed a bush to improve the view, and said if her father couldn't see Founders' Square now there was something wrong with him.

My mother was buried in The Roses Cemetery in Circleville, and she was surrounded by flowers. It was like a gentle meadow filled with color—perfect for a grower. Birds sang, a little stream flowed with clear water. People didn't march through The Roses at festival time because everyone came to Rock River, where the action was. That's why Dad chose it. Mother liked her privacy. In early spring she'd even tiptoed around her garden to not disturb her daffodil sproutings.

Nana had to go to town to decorate Grandpa's grave. Richard and I went with her because we had a heavy load of homework and were looking for anything to postpone the pain. Nana was sensible about death and didn't get emotional. She placed a huge basket of harvest flowers by his headstone, fixed it with a stake, and stamped her foot.

"If your grandpa were here he'd say that facing tough competition is what being a Morgan is all about, that bad weather is part of the growing life—you handle it and don't bellyache." Nana patted the headstone and looked straight at me. "That man was a lion when it came to being ornery."

Richard was uncomfortable in cemeteries, tried to look reverent, and spoke in hushed tones. He asked Nana if she wanted to sit with Grandpa for a while. Nana said good and loud that she'd sat with him for thirty-seven years and had better things to do.

We got pumpkin swirl ice cream from the 31 Flavors that was decked out with orange crepe paper and Indian corn. Outside on Marion Avenue, huge tables were being set up to hold the smaller pumpkin and squash entries that would start showing up Wednesday afternoon. By Wednesday the good food smells would float from homes and cottages as bakers perfected their prize pumpkin creations. Mannie Plummer would have tried and thrown out five batches of her pumpkin fudge because it always took Mannie seven tries to get it perfect. By Thursday morning at least 400 pumpkins, small to mammoth, would fill the avenue, circling the great scale Mrs. McKenna's grandfather had donated to the Weigh-In. 150,000 people would fill the streets of Rock River, anticipating The Great Moment.

I left Richard and Nana and stood before the scale where the Sweet Corn Coquette contestants would gather and wave in their yellow chiffon dresses. That contest would not take place until early February, but Bob Robertson of Robertson's Newsstand found that building up the anticipation was good for the contest and very good for business. I was not crazy about Max sharing the spotlight with Sharrell and her attendants. I was not happy that Big Daddy was completely hidden from view and not out fighting like a man. I missed Wes, who would probably miss the Weigh-In and forget all about me.

I touched the scale that would make or break my future and wilted under the terrible stress of competition. Everyone was counting on me. What if I didn't pull it off? "America doesn't do second place unless it's absolutely unavoidable," Gordon Mott had said.

A man was hammering a sign in place: "Here lie the greatest pumpkins in the world." I was getting nauseated. Nana pushed past me and threw her purse on the scale.

"Scale works," she said.

"I know it works, Nana."

"I figured you did. The hardest part is waiting."

"Tell me about it."

She sat down on an orange bench and motioned me over: "Know what's wrong with our world, Ellie?"

I fidgeted and sat. There was plenty wrong with it that I could see: war, famine, politics, Cyril.

"What's wrong with the world," Nana explained, "is that people stopped listening to their hearts."

Phil Urice was doing a little twirl in his pumpkin suit in Founders' Square. Frieda Johnson carried a brown and orange flowered wreath up the hill to the cemetery.

"Not everybody stopped listening," she continued, "but enough people did to make a difference. We've got so much in this life that all we know how to do is want more. So we concentrate on the wrong things—things we can see—as being the measure of a person. We think if we can win something big or buy something snazzy it'll make us more than we are. Our hearts know that's not true, but the eyes are powerful. It's easier to fix on what we can see than listen to the still, small voice of a whispering heart."

Nana turned her eyes on me like a vet looking for fleas: "A heart will say amazing things if it's given half a chance." She leaned into me now. "How many pumpkins you figure you've grown over the years?" she asked.

I considered this, counting back to my earliest squashes eight years ago. "Fifteen that I named," I said.

"Fifteen," Nana repeated. "Which one of them defines you as a person?"

I was about to say Max, of course, but stopped. I remembered working and learning in the fields as a kid, agonizing over each sprout that didn't make it, fighting like a cat for the ones that did, managing finally to grow Polly, my first thirty-pounder. Those were the battles that prepared me for growing giants; the giants before prepared me for growing Max.

"I guess they all define me, Nana."

"That's the right answer." Nana stood up. "Winning's a fine thing, Ellie, but it's all the months and years before and after that make you who you are." Nana patted my hand. "Grab hold of what your heart wants to tell you, honey, and you'll be one rich young woman."

We both got quiet. I pulled my coat tight and tried to listen to my heart. I heard something, all right: extreme pounding.

"You'll know when it's right," Nana said.

This was doubtful. I didn't know if I could even hang on till Thursday without melting my brain. I needed advice on *that.* "What's your suggestion on waiting these things out?" I groaned. "What do I do not to go crazy?"

Nana grabbed her purse off the scale and smiled

that smile that made her look like God's personal assistant. "You wait," she said.

I was hoping for something more concrete. "That's *it*? Aren't you going to tell me to get lost in a good book? Spend time with my friends to take my mind off the pressure? Pray? *Something?*"

The sun gave up and set behind 31 Flavors. Nana took my arm and we headed up Marion Avenue. "You *wait*," she said.

Chapter Twelve

I **was waiting.** Doing the things mature growers do to ease the stress of competition. I baked a batch of triple chocolate fudge bars and ate thirteen of them. I organized my baking pans. I had a one-hour phone call with Grace on the subject of when a woman starts going to pot. Grace said it was around thirty-five, when the lines started showing, but some, like her sister Ruth, could go much sooner. I pointed out that Aunt Peg was already forty-four, looked great, and in my opinion always would. Grace said that's because Aunt Peg had terrific cheekbones, which held her skin up. I counted the tiles on our bathroom walls (321). I counted the tiles on Nana's bathroom walls (266). I almost trained a pigeon to fetch a raisin and bring it back to me in its beak. I spent two hours writing a casual yet caring get-well note to Wes. I dusted off two books on General Patton, the closest I came to beginning my midterm paper. I asked Dad if I could be excused from homework. He told me not to push my luck.

Mrs. McKenna was lukewarm about my fame. On the one hand, any press coverage for the festival was good press; on the other, I was *only* sixteen, *only* beginning my life as a grower, unlike her friends Gloria Shack and Louise Carothers, who had been limping toward pumpkin celebrity for years and who, in my opinion, would never make it big. They were cowards who cut their pumpkins off the vine before a storm. They didn't have to listen to their hearts. They had Mrs. McKenna, who always took care of her friends, especially after the competition, when a decent-sized pumpkin could bring good money for its seeds. Growers knew that winning seeds spelled success. Gloria Shack and Louise Carothers sold their losing seeds at champion prices because Mrs. McKenna said *their* seeds had stood the test of time. I wouldn't sell Max's seeds for a million dollars because it would be like selling his children. Only a monster would do something like that.

I was not dealing with the pressure well and had started crying in school to relieve the stress. Richard said this was not good for my career because champions need to be composed in public even though they were cowards in real life. Gordon Mott's second article came out and made things worse. Justin made sure the whole school got a copy because Gordon Mott quoted two entire paragraphs from the *Defender*, and Justin was in journalistic heaven. I liked the first article better because it talked about squash tending and deep courage. The second article just talked about me, a subject I was getting pretty sick of. Justin grabbed me in the hall and said I must be very proud.

"I guess."

"*You guess?*" His eyebrows arched.

"It's okay."

"This"—Justin held Gordon Mott's article high— "is the best thing that has ever happened to Rock River, Ellie!"

I told Justin I was glad he was excited and I hoped he would win a Nobel prize someday. Justin didn't think journalists could win the Nobel prize.

"It doesn't matter," I said, walking away.

Justin said it did matter because winning the Nobel prize was a great honor. "I think," he shouted after me, "we can win it if we write about peace or disease!"

Two senior boys were drawing a mustache on the Thunderbird statue as I walked to my class. One of them put down his purple marker and shouted, "Way to go, Big Pumpkin Mama!" I sighed. My fans *were* everywhere.

I walked to phys ed good and slow. Before Ralphie, I was invisible in these halls. Before Ralphie, I would have given anything to be noticed and adored. Now I was stopped every two feet by someone, and it felt strange. Crash Bartwald and three defensive backs said hello and how was it go-go-going? Sharrell wiggled at me in greeting. The school nurse said I was looking pale and did I feel all right?

I didn't feel all right, I felt rotten. What if I lost? Then what? Would all these people still be my friends? Would Miss Moritz call me "a creative thinker who always brought something to class discussion" even though it was a dark, black lie that God would punish her for deeply?

I went to the school nurse's office with a pounding headache. She gave me Tylenol and said her whole family was rooting for me.

"I hope I won't let you down," I groaned.

The school nurse called Dad at his office, and he

140

came to take me home. She said I was going to be just fine and I owed it to all of Rock River to stay healthy.

Dad was worried as we pulled onto Bud DeWitt Memorial Drive, which had already been decorated with Frieda Johnson's orange and brown pumpkin road wreaths. We drove underneath the great sign: ROCK RIVER, IOWA, HOME OF AMERICA'S GREATEST PUMPKINS. Signs directing visitors to the festival grounds were everywhere, including one on the Backfarb Road turnoff that said: NO, NO . . . YOU'VE GONE TOO FAR. An orange line was painted down the drive. This was traditional and, as Nana said, really got folks in the mood for all the fun right there on the highway.

"I'm not sick," I said.

Dad looked at me. "You're a little pale, honey. We'll get you right home and—"

"I don't want to go home."

Dad pulled the car off the road. I looked down.

"I want to go see Mom."

That knocked Dad hard because we had only gone to visit her grave twice together. I'd been with Nana a few times and once with Aunt Peg. Dad got pretty emotional both times we went. He couldn't handle it, and neither could I.

"You mean now?"

"I want to get flowers first." Dad stared ahead quietly. "I need to do this," I said. "I need you to take me."

He nodded and started the engine. He seemed stooped and tired.

"I don't want to go to Frieda's," I said. "All she's got are those wreaths and pumpkin things. That's not right for—"

141

"No," Dad said. "I know the right place."

It was fifteen minutes to Circleville and Nielsen's Flower Garden, a big, glass greenhouse filled with potted flowers and hanging plants—a grower's place.

"Nothing orange," Dad said, making his way through the aisles with the young saleswoman. "Nothing phony."

We settled on a huge yellow mum plant in a basket. No bow. I held it on my lap as we drove past the Circleville bus stop where the commuter bus would run every two hours starting Thursday morning, delivering folks to the festival, since parking was impossible unless you were a friend of the mayor's. We pulled into The Roses Cemetery and followed the road to a little pond packed with ducks and swans. The swans were there, Dad had told me when I was younger, because they mate for life and never remarry. Dad stopped the car.

"Do you want me to go with you?" he asked.

"I need to go by myself."

The mum plant seemed heavy as I carried it past the rows of headstones to Mother's, which was by an oak tree with leaves just beginning to color. It was three o'clock. By this time tomorrow Harvest Eve would begin, the Christmas lights along Marion Avenue would light, spotlights would shine on lawn decorations, baking smells would pour from houses and shops.

Mother had died in November eight years ago, three weeks after the festival when Nana had won the blue ribbon for her upside-down rhubarb cake and cinched the best-all-around baking entry. Nana wasn't entering this year because she wanted to enjoy herself and not get crazy waiting for the judges to stop chewing and announce the winner. I put the basket down by

Mother's stone and sat in the grass as tears burned my eyes.

"Well," I finally said, "I'm having a pretty tough time." I'd never talked out loud at Mother's grave before, but this felt right.

"I have some stuff I need to talk to you about." I was crying heavy now and couldn't talk. I hung on to her stone and let the flood come. Nana said I'd cried like this at the funeral. I didn't remember. I was too busy shutting it out. I had screamed at the men who carried Mother's coffin out of the church to bring her back. They didn't.

Memories washed over me. I could see Dad's face when we came home that day—stony, cold, and gray—like he was dead, too. I remembered sleeping over at JoAnn's and watching her mother kiss her good night—I wanted her to kiss me, too—she was small and warm and smelled like flowers, but she patted my arm instead. I could see Nana pruning Mother's rose bushes to keep them full, teaching me how to cut back each stem with her clippers. When Dad and I moved Nana said she'd replant the roses in our new backyard, but Dad said no. It was too hard to remember.

A squirrel sniffed the mum. I was crying less now and tried again: "I know you were never much for competing, Mom, because Nana told me. I remember the roses you grew, though, I remember just about everything you grew, and I think if you'd tried to compete with them, you could have won."

The tears were coming again and I wiped them on my sleeve: "What I remember most about you, though, is how you loved the garden—how hard you worked to keep it beautiful. You always enjoyed it—whether it was a good year or an average one. I think I've lost the part about growing that I loved so much, Mother. The part I got from you and Nana. I'm so caught up in the winning, in being famous, that I'm not seeing too clear."

I said I was hurting and scared and didn't want to let anybody down. Winning had become so important it was making me sick. I was crying hard when Dad walked up beside me. His face was still.

"I decided," said Dad, "that I wanted to be here with you. Is that all right?" He handed me a handkerchief and sat on the grass. We held each other for a long time. I did most of the crying, but Dad got in his share.

"God, I miss her."

Dad whispered it and held me tight, and gradually we drew strength from each other, like Max pulled nourishment from the earth. It made me feel locked into Dad, like a little pumpkin growing from a big vine. I handed him back his handkerchief.

"You have more of your mother in you than you know, Ellie," he said finally. I shook my head. I couldn't see it. "Yes, you do," he insisted. "And it's a wonderful thing she gave you."

I sniffed.

"You can find quietness and beauty in difficult times. You have an amazing love and dedication to growing, although I know you think you've lost that. You haven't, honey."

"Yes, I have."

"You've done something fine with Max, and you should be terribly proud. You can't stop now. Your mother would tell you that because it was her favorite speech to me." His face went soft, like he was remembering something precious.

"I don't feel I'm . . . worthy . . . you know? All the attention doesn't seem—"

"Justified?"

"I feel all messed up, Dad."

Dad put his arm around me. "You are," he said, "the toughest person I know. You have fire and life and courage. You and Max have captured the heart of this town with talent and raw determination. If anybody deserves to win, it's you."

I wiped my eyes. "You think I deserve to win?"

"Yes, I do."

"You don't think it's wrong to want to win this bad? Or that I'm too young and should have suffered more?"

Dad laughed. "I think you've suffered enough." That was good to hear. I didn't think I could take much more.

"I just want to interject here, Dad, that I might not win. Cyril's pumpkin is as big as Cleveland."

"And Max," Dad said, "is as big as Cincinnati."

I smiled at this great truth as Mother's yellow mum stretched to grow.

"Stand up," he ordered. "You inherited my stubbornness."

I stood, sensing Dad's unmovable drive. I took the handkerchief back and blew my nose.

"I reject all past negative programming," Dad boomed.

"I reject all past negative programming," I said back.

"I believe in myself," we said together, but I stopped. This didn't seem right.

"I can't, Dad. I don't feel those words like you do." He was quiet. "I've always tried to say them when you wanted me to, but—"

"I've seen this work, Ellie—thousands of times. . . ."

"I need to find the courage myself."

The Circleville Bell Tower struck five and echoed through the quiet cemetery. I looked hard at Mother's grave. Dad looked, too, and heaved a sigh so deep you'd think he'd dropped a piano.

"All right," he said finally. "I respect that."

There was something in those words that broke new ground, like a seed growing shoots and pushing through topsoil. A peace floated down and covered our hearts. We waited for a while, then Dad took my arm and we walked to the car together like a real family.

Back home, Dad and I measured Max from stem to nose horizontally around his fattest part. He had pushed out 8½ more inches in the past three days, which I estimated was good for another 35 pounds. This put him over 600 big ones, a champion in anybody's book. Nobody had even seen a pumpkin over 500 pounds before 1984, and here we were in the big time within spitting distance of colossal. Max could have snagged a hundred pumpkin contests if it hadn't been for Big Daddy hiding in the shadows. Max had been gaining good weight, just like Wes told him. His skin was darker, too—a clear sign he was ripe and ready for cutting.

I missed Wes. He was supposed to help me cut Max off the vine, and now I'd have to do it alone. He called, sniffling and coughing, to report his fever had finally broken, but Dr. Buntz said his sinuses still looked like Jell-O and pronounced the curse: He was stuck in bed till Friday. No Weigh-In. He'd miss it all. By Friday the world would know whether I was a winner or just a flash in the patch. Dr. Buntz had the soul of a turnip. Wes said he was thinking deep thoughts in Max's direction, which, I told him, were absolutely working. He said he'd gotten my note. *He said he missed me* and sneezed twice. I told him I missed him, too, and hung up shaking.

He missed me. That meant I was missable. Like the lady in the perfume commercial whose smell sticks in the guy's head as he pictures her running along the beach barefoot. I wondered how Wes thought about me. We hadn't been to the beach yet and wouldn't be going until I lost ten more pounds. The last time I ran on a beach barefoot I stepped on a broken beer bottle and had to get seven stitches. Probably he remembered me patting compost around Max's belly. Not exactly commercial material, but for a grower, it would do.

Spider came up and licked my hand. Richard was returning him to the Ankers tomorrow, a new dog, if I did say so myself. He'd stopped barking at absolutely everything and only shrieked when the noise had it coming, like when the raccoon that drove Mrs. Lemming crazy was out behind her garbage can making a racket. In less than two weeks Spider had become a sophisticated dog of the world. We had taught him to sit, sort of, we had introduced him to gourmet food and classical music. We hadn't killed him.

Spider stood by the door watching the patch, his head cocked in disbelief. I looked outside and saw a true miracle. I moved to the porch to get a better look and still couldn't believe it. There knelt Old Abe in the dirt, tape recorder in hand, next to Max.

"Max," Dad began, "I'm about to play you one of the greatest inspirational pieces of music ever written, filled with triumph and greatness. I want you to rise up when you hear it. Rise up and achieve your full potential! Is that clear?"

A wind blew Max's leaves, and Dad stood triumphantly. Music! I'd never thought of that! He pressed his tape recorder, and the sounds of Handel's *Messiah* filled the patch.

"Yes!" Dad shouted, turning the volume louder. The sopranos were going at it, hitting all the high notes. Spider was howling with the altos. The basses were doing whatever basses do against the melody. "And he shall reign forever and ever!" they sang. It was just like a movie. I half expected Moses to come down from a mountain and part the Rock River, but given its size that wouldn't have been much of a trick. Max filled with splendor as the million choir voices rang "Hallelujah!"

"Reach for it!" Dad cried.

"Yes!" I shouted.

"Reach for it!" Dad cried again.

I reached for it, tripped over Spider, who was yelping at my feet, and landed facedown in a mound of pearlite.

Chapter Thirteen

I slept badly—a total of two hours and seventeen minutes, typical for Harvest Eve. A small shaft of light had hit the sky and was trying to break through to dawn. It was quiet and still, like a church on Monday morning. I listened for the October wind stirring in the patch and felt an old sadness. I picked up my thick-bladed cleaver and walked outside to wait for Nana and Richard and something else I didn't want to think about.

It was time to cut Max off the vine.

Ordinarily, this was a big moment for a grower. Gloria Shack said it was like cutting a baby's umbilical cord and watching it start life on its own. Ha! A baby's got years ahead of it. A squash cut off the vine won't last more than eight weeks and starts losing weight the same day. It was the beginning of the end, that's all.

I sat in the patch trying to imagine what it would be like without Max. He was so much a part of me. My friend. My vegetable. You can't just turn that off. Max's stem was fat and dry and beginning to wither: He was perfectly ripe. I hid my cleaver behind my back as a sparrow sang a funeral march in a nearby elm.

Nana and Richard pulled up, and the procession began. Dad came out in his bathrobe, Richard carried his mitt out of respect. Nana held something in a Ziploc bag close to her chest. They walked solemnly toward Max. I produced the knife.

"This is going to sting a little."

Richard gasped. The sparrow gave me a dirty look. I lifted it high—Ellie the Ripper—and hacked through his stem with three smooth swipes, leaving four inches intact. Max's vine flopped on the ground. I rubbed his cut and bowed my head at the injustice of agricultural death.

Phil Urice, dressed in his pumpkin suit, and his three-hundred-pound brother, Bomber, backed a pickup covered with orange flags and flapping harvest streamers into the patch.

"Gonna give Cyril a run for his money with this one," Phil said, fixing a rubber pad the size of a blanket under Max. The four men grabbed a corner. Bomber pushed, his muscles bulged, Dad shoved, Richard pulled, Phil sweated. "Here she goes!" hollered Phil, and with a grunt, Max was lifted onto the truck—a liberated squash. I climbed in beside him and tucked a blanket around his base. It was a great honor to ride to the fair with the official Rock River Dancing Pumpkin, and I figured Phil's clout could only help my chances. Nana threw the Ziploc bag in my lap.

"A present," she announced. The bag had a clump of moist soil inside. Nana crossed her arms and looked at me hard. "Four generations of Morgans worked that soil to get it how it is, sweating themselves silly in the field, and I don't want you messing things up by thinking that winning today is more important than that."

I gulped and nodded.

"You grew your first pumpkin in it and your father tilled it when he was a boy even though he hated every minute. It's going to be here long after all of us are gone, and if you think one Weigh-In makes a whale of a difference to who you are, then you'd better think again, that's all. Any questions?"

This was not the supportive farewell I had expected. And as for questions, I had plenty. Beginning with how you turn off winning when you want it so bad and how come nobody seemed to have an answer for *that*? I stared at the bag. "No questions," I said.

"Well, then, off you go."

Phil backed out of the patch real easy. Nana'd calmed down and was grinning like a true blue-ribbon champion, Richard and Dad waved good-bye as the truck rolled down the driveway. I didn't have the heart to tell Max that a pumpkin was not forever, tucked the Ziploc bag under his blanket, and settled in for the ride to town.

Cyril Pool had not arrived at the fairgrounds despite the fact that all growers had to be in their places by 9:00 A.M. *sharp* or be subject to extreme penance and deep anguish. Mrs. McKenna glared down Marion Avenue for any sign of his truck, swallowed three Extra-Strength Excedrins, and folded her arms like an evil genie. Cyril was dead meat. Ha-ha.

It wasn't like Cyril to miss an opportunity to be a degenerate. He always came early to stick it to other growers about how big his pumpkin was and how measly theirs were. Maybe God had taken pity on me and Big Daddy's rot had gotten the best of him. Maybe God had sent plague and destruction Cyril's way. Maybe Mrs. McKenna had disqualified Cyril for bad taste and nastiness. I hoped God had chosen plague and destruction, since they tend to have long-range effects.

A baseball flopped inside Phil's truck. Richard followed. "Cyril's been delayed," he said. "Had a little problem getting Big Daddy on the trailer."

I leaned forward: "*What* little problem?"

"He doesn't have enough men to lift Big Daddy on the truck. Not too popular."

This was not exactly plague and destruction, but it was still decent news. All pumpkin entries must be in by 10:00 A.M. or be disqualified. It was nine thirty-five already.

Maybe . . .

Richard jumped out as Gordon Mott's head peered over the side: "Kid, you have to give it more pizzazz. Trust me on this."

"I'm feeling the pressure, Mr. Mott, and—"

"Do you have any clue who's here today, kid?"

I didn't.

"A reporter from the *Chicago Tribune*. Flown direct from O'Hare Airport at great expense to cover your story. Why, you might ask yourself, is she here?"

"Because you invited her."

"I didn't *invite* her, kid. All I did was tell her the story line." He stared off into the blue sky and lifted his

hands to the clouds: "Teenager risks all to gain pumpkin glory." He relaxed his face and watched me long and
hard. "You've got to have heart today. You've got to be
sharp, savvy."

"I'll try—"

Gordon Mott leaned forward and gave me the wisdom of the publishing world. "Everybody wants a hero.
Somebody honest, hardworking, looking toward a no-
bler purpose. Somebody they can put their hopes and
dreams in who won't let them down. Like Shirley
Temple—a great kid, great orphan roles—everybody
loves an overcomer. Astronauts did what everybody
wanted to and looked good coming out of the cone in the
water. Barbie dolls had style, didn't mouth off, and they
were cheaper than a new bike, at least in the beginning.
Now you and the vegetable have that same role model
quality. Are you following me?"

"I'm not sure."

"I've seen them come," Gordon Mott said, "and I've
seen them go. The great ones have a simple appeal. I
think you and the vegetable have it. Relax, kid. Life's
tough enough." I tensed.

"What," I asked, "if I don't win?"

"Network news wouldn't touch it. You'd get a couple of paragraphs in some local dailies, maybe a side
panel in one of the farm rags, but I wouldn't hold my
breath."

I tried to digest what Gordon Mott was saying.
A toddler ran by with a sign clipped to his wind-
breaker: BILL SUDD'S GRANDCHILD. PLEASE
RETURN. Reunited families dressed in orange
strolled arm in arm.

"You want me," I said, "to be the next Barbie doll?"

He looked at me and, of course, I didn't qualify. I tossed back my hair, sucked in my stomach, and shoved out my chest.

"Not technically, kid," he said. "You can only go with what you've got."

"You think I could be a role model?"

A bug flew into my mouth and I spat it out. Disgusting.

Gordon Mott regarded my spit on the ground. "With a little work," he said, and walked toward the pumpkin fudge table.

Suddenly, a truck horn blasted loud and off-key. My heart sank to my shoes because without looking *I knew.* I turned, and here he came in all his glory— Cyril Pool—four-time blue-ribbon winner standing in his open-back trailer with all his ribbons pinned to his chest. Herman was at the wheel, spitting and grinning. Cyril was waving a big American flag like an Olympic athlete ready to grab the gold medal. He'd even bathed. Next to him was Big Daddy, wrapped in padding and blankets for the trip, but enough of him showed to make the crowd go, "Ahhhhhhh." I told Max not to look.

"Guess he fixed the problem." It was Richard.

Mrs. McKenna did not like being upstaged. She raised her bullhorn and blasted him: "This is deplorable, Mr. Pool! I hope you're good and ashamed of yourself for being tardy, because *we* certainly are ashamed of you!"

Cyril dropped his flag and said, "Well, Missy, I'm here now, ain't I?"

She eyed him with contempt. "In place, Pool!"

Mannie Plummer was in charge of check-in. She came to Cyril. "Take the blankets off, please."

"Not jus' yet," Cyril snarled.

"People would like to see the pumpkin. That's why we have a festival."

"When I'm good and ready."

Mannie wrote "Present, but ornery" by Cyril's number and moved forward to Gloria Shack.

"Something's up," I said to Richard. "Cyril's acting weird."

Cyril was picking his teeth and slobbering a bit on his ribbons. Acting weird was within the range of normal for him. "He's a strange man, Ellie."

"Not that. Something's up with Big Daddy. Look how he's got him covered."

"Five minutes to fair time, people!" Mrs. McKenna blared. "Let's put on our happy Harvest faces."

Sharrell clicked into gear at this, beaming and waving. Not to be outdone, the other Sweet Corn Coquettes grinned and squealed. Cyril Pool did not have a happy Harvest face—his was darkening by the minute. He pulled the padding around Big Daddy and stuffed mounds of hay under his base. He was nervous and quiet, not the old Cyril Pool Rock River loved to hate.

"Hey, Cyril!" cried a man in the crowd. "Let's see what kind of pumpkin you got there!" But Cyril shook his head and pulled the covering tighter.

I was beginning to get a good idea what kind of pumpkin he had there. A questionable one, that's what. Deep, spreading rot on a pumpkin is not a pretty sight. Still, Cyril had gotten Big Daddy on the trailer. That meant the pumpkin was in one piece. That meant it was weighable. And that meant I was probably dead.

"It's no use," I said miserably.

Richard threw down his glove: "Look at you! You're not even at the scale yet, and you've already lost!"

"Big Daddy is bigger, Richard! There's nothing I can do about—"

The muscles in Richard's neck were sticking out like they did whenever Mr. Soboleski replaced him in the outfield. "Give yourself a break, Ellie!" He sat down. He stood up. "People come from behind and *win*! It happens!"

"Max isn't going to get any bigger, Richard!"

Richard glared at me: "It's not over till it's over!" He stamped his foot: "It ain't over till the fat lady sings!" He was snarling now: "Win one for the Gipper!"

"Squash 'em!" Dad's voice rang out. He was standing by the truck, towering above the masses. "Squash 'em!" Old Abe shouted it again, smiled at the crowd, and zapped them with motivation.

"Squash 'em!" a boy yelled.

"Squash 'em!" Grace shouted. "Beat his pants off, Ellie, you can do it!" Max seemed to rise in greatness. I was standing straight now as the cry rang like a chorus of hope.

Click. Gordon Mott stepped from the shouting mob very pleased indeed. Click. At his side was a photographer in a *Chicago Tribune* sweatshirt clicking his camera like he couldn't get enough. Click. I gave him my right side. Click. Max did a little jig. Click. The woman next to Gordon Mott and the photographer was smiling and nodding and writing furiously on a pad as the cheer of "Squash 'em!" echoed across Main Street, bounced off the Bud DeWitt Memorial White Hen and right into Big Daddy's dirty, rotten core. Click. Gordon Mott smiled at me with headlines in his eyes. Click.

"Silence, people, please!"

Mrs. McKenna held her pruning shears high and waited until we obeyed. Parents hushed children. Feet moved into respectful position. She cut the great orange ribbon in front of the Bud DeWitt Memorial White Hen and threw up her arms. "Let the festival begin!" she cried, and almost got trampled as the crowds ran to the food tables up and down Marion Avenue.

Chapter Fourteen

I was standing by the 31 Flavors Harvest Turkey absolutely dripping with heart and pizzazz when Grace slapped a sealed envelope in my hand that read "Deliver to Ellie/Personal and Confidential."

"From Wes," she said. "He's my cousin and I have a right to know what's inside."

This was debatable. "Personal and Confidential" pretty much meant that, and if Wes had dragged himself from his sickbed to contact me, it had to be important. I yawned like I got envelopes every day and backed off fast, smack into Frieda Johnson's cinnamon syrup bun table, almost knocking her tub of hand-cranked maple butter to its death. Frieda glared at me like I was an alien, so I snuck between the pumpkin sloppy joe stand and the pumpkin doughnut table and ripped The Letter open. It started with "Dear Ellie," which meant he cared:

"I bet you weren't expecting to hear from me to-day. Well, I wasn't expecting to write you either, but I guess this flu's got me for a while longer, although I hate to admit that, not ever being sickly."

Grace was moving in for heavy spying. I spun around past the pumpkin and sausage stew line and read fast: "I've been thinking about you and Max and how you probably need a pep talk right now. I want to say that I'm proud to know both of you because it takes guts to come this far. And, Ellie, you've got more guts than any girl I've ever known."

My heart was clicking because I knew for certain that The Other One in Gaithersville had fewer guts and was definitely dead and buried. Ha-ha. Grace was tiptoeing up from behind—I dashed behind the Amana Colonies' sauerbraten and spaetzle corner and kept reading: "Now, I want you to put aside everything you know about growing for a minute. I want you to stop thinking about Cyril Pool and where you are and how you feel because the best piece of advice I can give you from competing at fairs myself is don't look at the competition, just concentrate on yourself. If you look at Cyril you'll just get mad, and that makes everything worse. If you listen to your nerves, they'll take over. So just remember who you are. Once that starts flowing there's no telling what can happen. And stop thinking about winning as beating Cyril, because there's a lot more to growing giant pumpkins than that.

"I guess I'll let you go and let you get concentrating. I miss you and believe in you."

He had underlined his name, and I got all quiet inside, like I'd found a secret place in a forest nobody knew about. I held the greatest inspirational message of the twentieth century over my heart, filled with deep truth and courage from the past president of the

Gaithersville Ag Club, and faced the giant scale. I stared at it until it was energized with a picture of Max sliding on with one humongous plop, the weight of him pushing it to its limit, my hands lifted in a great winning moment.

Cyril, sensing my new power, was hissing at people to keep away from his trailer. I turned away because Wes had said not to look and concentrated on not being nervous. This is hard to do when your heart is beating in your kidneys. Richard said eating was the key to peace and there was enough food at the fair to keep anybody mellow. Dad said going on a ride would take my mind off things, but I thought puking from the side of the Mad Screaming Bomber could make me lose my competitive edge.

I found a pay phone to call Wes to tell him how much I appreciated The Letter and how I was concentrating my brains out, which was the least I could do for the cause of agriculture and teenagers in America. No one answered. This got me worried, because he could have taken a turn for the worse and be *at this moment* rushing to a hospital for who knows what. He could also be sleeping. Grace said Wes slept like a brick.

Miss Moritz walked by holding hands with a man who looked like General Patton (which meant she was part human) when Gordon Mott slipped beside me.

"You're looking good, kid. Looking strong."

He was eating a fat bratwurst covered with grilled red onions on an onion roll. He smiled at the *Chicago Tribune* reporter several yards away, who nodded. "She's just going to watch you for a while, kid. That's her style. Think bigger than life."

"This really isn't me, Mr. Mott, I—"

But he was gone—in a flash of bratwurst and onions. Who was that masked man?

It was 1:45 P.M. I had made three calls to Wes and gotten no answer. I had eaten three of Frieda Johnson's cinnamon syrup buns, two bowls of pumpkin sausage stew, a slice of pumpkin pie, and gotten heartburn. The seams of my khaki slacks were close to exploding. I sat in the truck with Max, polishing him with a soft cloth, holding Nana's Ziploc bag, remembering the agricultural blood that flowed through my veins. All growers had to be in their trucks by now and check in with Mannie Plummer, who let everyone know that she would have been sitting in her truck with her pumpkin if Ralphie or Dennis hadn't shaken hands with the devil and ruined her life. I was about to let loose a great flow of winning concentration that would have made Wes proud when it happened.

I looked.

Not at Cyril. At Big Daddy. I looked at Big Daddy in his extreme hugeness, and all that agricultural heritage that was holding me together went splat. I tried to recover, but Big Daddy's leer was carved in my memory, and it was no use.

He was bigger.

I slumped over Max like a runner who'd looked over her shoulder and lost the race.

Max couldn't win.

Big Daddy was the biggest pumpkin I'd ever seen and it was no use kidding myself anymore. I buried Nana's Ziploc bag under Max's blanket and sat in second-place straw.

Mannie approached Cyril's trailer.

"Okay, Mr. Pool," Mannie began, reaching for the blanket that covered Big Daddy. "No more excuses. Uncover your squash, please."

Cyril snorted and Herman blew a wad out his mouth. "Well now, Missy," he said. "What'n if I ain't ready?"

"Then, Mr. Pool," said Mannie, eyeing Cyril like an Orkin man looks at a rat, "you will be disqualified."

"Says who?"

Mannie pointed to her extremely official name tag with the gold lettering that said OFFICIAL PUMPKIN WEIGH-IN COORDINATOR. She leaned toward Cyril, her eyes on fire: "In this line I'm the law, mister!"

The smaller pumpkins under a hundred pounds were being weighed—the Small Sugars, Sweet Spookies, and Lady Godivas. The crowd applauded politely as each entry slid onto the scale. Hugh Ferguson backed his truck up to the starting gate. I was number 96.

Mannie was steaming. "The blanket comes off now," she spat, "or you're out!"

A small crowd was gathering around Cyril's trailer. The sheriff moved to Mannie's side and put his hand on his gun. "Well," Cyril complained, "ain't you all makin' a big fuss over a little question?"

"Got to obey the rules, Cyril," said the sheriff, "if you're going to play in the game."

Mannie nodded. Richard thumped his mitt. "I'm gonna play," Cyril said, lifting the blanket slowly to reveal a perfectly shaped pumpkin with a three-foot dark area along its side and top. "I'm gonna win!"

Big Daddy glared at the crowd, which was hushed by his greatness. Max seemed to wither beside me. Mannie took off her glasses and pointed to the dark area.

162

"Bruise," explained Cyril.

"That's a mighty big bruise," Mannie observed, reaching to touch it. "Looks more like—"

Cyril pushed her hand away. "No touchin'," he said.

Suddenly a hacking voice rang out: "That pumpkin's not in any shape to compete, ma'am!"

Heads turned toward the voice who stepped from behind the giant scale. Mannie lowered her clipboard. The sheriff pushed back his hat. Cyril's face froze as Wes walked forward, red-nosed, a wad of tissues in his hand. He glanced at me quickly and let Cyril have it.

"You've got a squash full of rot there, Mr. Pool! In Gaithersville they'd never let you put that thing on the scale. No, sir!"

Mannie dropped the number 94 she was going to slap on Cyril's trailer. Wes blew his nose. Nothing like this had ever happened in Rock River. Not ever. It was wonderful. Wes was wonderful.

Cyril rose, his nostrils spitting fire. "Jus' who you think you are?"

"President of the Gaithersville Agricultural Club, remember, Mr. Pool? I know pumpkins, and I say yours is a goner. Nothing personal."

"You're a dirty liar, boy!" But Cyril was sweating good. Mannie and Mrs. McKenna started whispering. Four burly men slid Hugh Ferguson's lopsided pumpkin onto a blanket and onto the great scale: 288 pounds. Hugh grinned. The crowd applauded. The giant Weigh-In had begun.

Mayor Clint joined the people gathered around Mannie. Wes stood his ground, looking gorgeous, coughing with style. Cyril snarled at Wes and covered Big Daddy with a blanket. Helen Bjork's squash hit

222, a disappointing showing. Nine heads were in a huddle. Justin Julee appeared. "Ellie," he whispered, "do you have a comment on all this?"

I glanced at Wes, who was wonderful and brave and exciting even when he sneezed, which was a real test of a person's charisma. "No comment," I said.

Justin climbed over Max into the truck. "Come on, Ellie. Do you think Cyril Pool should be disqualified?"

This was an excellent question, one I'd been considering for years. Justin was champing at the bit, so I said, "I think any grower should be disqualified who tries to compete with a squash filled with rot and disease."

Justin wrote this furiously. "Do you think," he began, but was silenced as Mrs. McKenna and Mannie stepped forward. "We feel the young man has a point, Mr. Pool," Mannie began.

"He's got nuthin'!" Cyril snarled.

"This," continued Mannie, "is a fair assembly, sir, and you'd better listen up." Cyril sniffed hard and kicked the trailer. "We want to be fair, since you have been this festival's winner four years running, but we must also consider the other contestants."

Wes moved closer to Max, grinning like a man with a wonderful secret: "Max, you're the greatest pumpkin in the world and I want you to start acting like it. Don't you look at Big Daddy and get one bit nervous. Don't look at him at all, Max. You just concentrate on that scale and breaking it when they roll you on. You're two hundred pounds bigger than a tiger, Max, and there's no vegetable in the entire vegetable kingdom that can make that claim because a pumpkin is king and always was. The biggest cabbage was only a hundred twenty-one pounds; the biggest gourd was only a hundred ninety-six. I saw a two-hundred-sixty-pound water-melon once, and it wasn't much. A seven-pound tomato, a thirty-six-pound zucchini, these vegetables don't get me excited. Ellie gave you everything she's got—that's why you're here. She's why I'm here, too. You're a scale-buster, Max. I'm proud to know you."

Wes nodded his head because he was through, and if I hadn't been a girl with deep guts and extreme courage I would have fainted right there. I grabbed hold of Max's stem as Wes sneezed like a world-class champion.

"Holding up okay?" he asked.

I nodded because I figured a nod was less of a lie.

"The committee," Mannie announced, "will examine your squash, Mr. Pool, and decide if it is fit for competition."

Cyril narrowed his beady eyes: "You ain't got no right—"

Mrs. McKenna was on him like an angry bee. "One more outburst, Pool, and you're out. For good! Take it or leave it!"

Gloria Shack's pumpkin slid onto the scale and hit 428 even. The crowd cheered. Cyril fingered each blue ribbon on his shirt. "I'll take it," he snarled. "But you ain't gonna find nuthin'."

"We'll see," said Mannie. She rolled up her sleeves and led the committee of nine to the trailer and Big Daddy.

Chapter Fifteen

A **cloud had fallen** on Rock River and divided the town. The nice folks were on my side, the cranky ones went with Cyril. Founders' Square was thick with grumbling people, and the committee was making things worse. There were no bylaws about rotting entries, no rules on deep treachery and deceit. Grown-ups sure could muck things up. Mannie was hollering at the mayor, who was hollering at the sheriff, who hollered that Spears could just shoot Big Daddy and that would be the end of it. Grace shouted that teenagers everywhere should unite against the tyranny of adult oppression. Dad cornered the entire committee and loudly objected to everything. Mrs. McKenna's voice rose above the giant scale: "We will not make any decisions like this, people!"

Wes spoke right back to her in extreme wonderfulness: "Seems to me, Aunt Adelaide, there's only one decision to make. No disrespect intended." We waited, hushed by his courage. Mrs. McKenna let him live.

The Weigh-In continued as the giant pumpkins rolled on the scale. Number 22. Number 23. Flat, skinny, some downright ugly, but you'd never know it by watching the growers' faces.

Wes held my hand in front of Dad, who played it real easy, like I had boys around all the time. JoAnn said I was lucky, and she should know. Her father specialized in fear, being a life insurance salesman, and could bring a boy to his knees.

"May I have your attention, please?"

It was Oral Perkins, of Oral Perkins Chevrolet, a big-time festival supporter who donated three Chevy Cavaliers to be raffled off every year and who had an extremely big "in" with Mrs. McKenna. He stood on the oratory contest podium—a mean man with a mission.

"I think," his voice declared, "we're wasting time. This is an *adult* Weigh-In!" He glared at me because he only connected with car buyers. "Pool's got a pumpkin. We've got the scale. Let's get on with it!"

He backed away to tense applause as Wes tore up the podium steps and stood tall and proud like a true candidate of the little people: "Ellie Morgan," he shouted, "has been accepted into this *adult* division fair and square! Ellie Morgan kept control of her pumpkin and fought off rot to bring him to this Weigh-In as a clean competitor. She's grown a pumpkin bigger than most of us will ever see, and to let a rotting pumpkin beat her, even one grown by a four-time blue-ribbon winner—well, sir, that's just not fair!"

My heart thunked in deep, cosmic love as Rock River High rose cheering, stomping, and belching in a great show of unity and disgust for authority. I thought I heard a familiar voice, and I looked. There stood Miss Moritz *on the podium*! No! About to tell the entire town that I hadn't turned in my midterm paper. I grabbed my throat, hoping my scream for mercy would carry in time. Miss Moritz aimed. I couldn't watch.

"History," she cried, "teaches us many lessons." Miss Moritz paused here for total effect, like she did in class. "*What* lessons, you might ask?"

I wasn't going to ask. I didn't want to know, although I had a pretty good idea.

"History is our friend. We can trust its message. We must," she was shouting now, "listen to its message!" The crowd was listening but not getting it, which also happened to Miss Moritz's students when she spoke. "The history of this Weigh-In is its commitment to excellence, is it not?" No one answered her. "You can't all be sleeping!"

Hugh Ferguson raised his hand and said, yes, the history of the Weigh-In was its commitment to excellence.

She pointed to the great sign: HERE LIE THE GREATEST PUMPKINS IN THE WORLD. "Does Mr. Pool's squash belong under that sign?" The crowd turned to the sign and shivered. "Does a partially rotting pumpkin winner continue this Weigh-In's great tradition of excellence?"

"No!" shouted a woman.

"Not at this festival!" cried another.

"I rest my case," said Miss Moritz. She walked off the stage and into the waiting arms of the winner of the General Patton look-alike contest. I searched for a pad and paper to start work on my midterm but came up dry.

"You know that woman?" It was the *Tribune* reporter.

"She's one of my teachers."

"You like her?"

Wes was at my side: "She does now."

Oral Perkins was frowning and whispered something to Mrs. McKenna, who nodded and stormed the podium.

"I have an announcement from the committee!"

A crying baby was rushed away by its parents. A good thing, since Mrs. McKenna would have probably had it shot. Rock River held its breath.

"It is," she declared, "the decision of the committee that Cyril Pool's pumpkin is perfectly fit for competition."

I slumped against Max, who lost five pounds right there. Anger and applause ripped through the crowd. Dad threw down his hat and demanded a retrial. Gordon Mott threw down his Hunan pumpkin with minced pork. Wes grabbed my hand. Cyril whooped and tossed hay in the air.

"That," Mrs. McKenna directed, "is final. We will continue the weighing."

With that, Adelaide McKenna, the Meanest Woman in America, walked off the podium and through the crowd, who parted for her in silence—except for Mannie Plummer, who stood her ground. Mannie said this never would have happened if Bud DeWitt was still alive. It was a dark, dark day in Rock River, Iowa.

It was night. The spotlights made a yellow blur as Louise Carothers stood by her pumpkin screaming

169

that if anyone dropped it there'd be trouble. The scale read 471 pounds, and the weigher cried out the number like he was sick of the whole thing. A mime juggled oranges and dropped two on a little girl's foot. Mayor Clint gave a short speech about Bud DeWitt, which was usually good for a standing ovation, but only a few people clapped, and those who did didn't mean it.

The magic was gone.

"I'm Number One! I'm Number One!"

Cyril was strutting around his trailer as Herman backed it into position. I huddled around Max with family and friends and wondered why bad things happened to good pumpkins.

People gathered at the side of Phil Urice's truck like a funeral line about to view a body, stretching halfway down the block. Nana watched me, and I couldn't meet her gaze.

"Cyril Pool!" cried the weigher. "Number Ninety-four!"

It had to happen. I tried not to look as Cyril paraded from his trailer patting all his ribbons, but I did look, and tears stung my eyes. I shook my head to stop them, telling myself it didn't matter. There was always next year.

Cyril grabbed an end of the blanket as Phil and Bomber Urice pushed the huge pumpkin from the hay.

"Easy, boys!" Cyril shouted. "I said easy now!"

I shut my eyes, but the tears wouldn't give up. I had to pull myself together, not cry in the straw like a second-place jerk. I looked at Nana for one shaky second and she looked back with all the strength in heaven and zapped it into me.

My hands shot under Max's blanket and grabbed

the Ziploc bag with that clump of black, moist earth. My great-grandfather tilled it and my father worked it and my grandmother used it to grow magic. My cousins hoed it and my uncle stomped it down and my mother planted a rose bush in it that shot to the sky like a bright yellow miracle. There wasn't any soil energized with more love and perspiration that God had ever created.

The four men around Big Daddy were joined by a fifth, then another. "Hoist him, boys," said Phil Urice, "on three. One." The men moved Big Daddy higher. "Two." Cyril was screaming they'd better be careful or he'd have their hides.

I ripped open the bag and shoved my hands inside, squeezing the soil through my fingers. I remembered Mother's hands, which were always dark from the earth, and how she loved that garden, whether it was a good year or an average one.

Phil Urice hollered "Three!"

Big Daddy slid onto the great scale with a grunt.

The Cyril people were applauding, the Ellie people were booing. I closed my eyes and listened to my heart.

I remembered who I was.

"Six hundred sixty-eight point two pounds!" cried the weigher. "A new Harvest Fair record!"

Mrs. McKenna congratulated Cyril, who was bowing like a big creep, but somehow it didn't matter near as much as I would have figured.

That's when Nana elbowed me.

"Get ready, honey," she laughed. "Something's moving in the air."

I looked, and something was happening because the weigher said, "Hold on now!" I wasn't close enough to see, but Richard was. He stepped to the scale, shouted, "Yee-ha!" and threw his mitt in the air. Dad ran over and stared at Big Daddy, who sat huge and mean—so much of him that a few inches hung over the scale.

"What's that?" asked several in the crowd, pointing to Big Daddy's bottom. Mrs. McKenna's hand froze in midair. Oral Perkins's mouth was open like a dead fish's.

There was a gurgle. Then a shake. And like a bolt from heaven, like all the badness and rottenness that was inside Cyril and the way he'd treated every grower within two hundred miles just couldn't be contained. It was like a hundred Fourth of Julys all rolled into one, better than the best fireworks that had ever shot into the sky, better than sitting with a champion squash in the moonlight holding the hand of the one you love.

There was so much of it, it just couldn't stop. All that bad that was in Cyril had gotten into Big Daddy—formed right there good and heavy at his base—and like all badness, it couldn't stay hidden forever. Sooner or later it had to come out, and it was coming out now. Starting to seep—thick, orange, smelly muck—dribbling out of Big Daddy's dark spot for all the world to see.

"Step back!" the weigher cried.

"Thank you, Lord," said Nana.

And that ooze was gaining strength, like the Rock River when it was really something to see, when the water just kept flowing downhill, past rocks and turns, moving faster and faster. Out the orange glop came, moving like white water. Someone had turned on a waterspout. There was so much of it, it started running down the scale, dropping to the street below, falling thick and rotten in a big puddle right there on Marion Avenue and stunk like old meat. Cyril ran to his pumpkin and tried to patch him up, like the little boy who put his finger in the dam, but it was too late. That pumpkin started shrinking, the rot had pushed down to the base and Big Daddy's sides were hanging over the scale. It was a great moment in pumpkin history.

"She's going to blow!" called the weigher.

"Yes!" shouted Wes.

Yes! I shouted inside, but couldn't speak. I couldn't move. But I didn't have to do anything.

There was a rumble and a heave. The shell that was Big Daddy cracked from the bottom to the top and rivers of rotten orange liquid sprayed down the scale and across the heads of the people closest up. They backed off disgusted, wiping the gunk from their clothes. Then the top that was Big Daddy heaved once, twice, and collapsed like my first chocolate soufflé, pushing more glop down the great scale Mrs. McKenna's grandfather donated to the festival in 1953.

Dad started laughing, the way he used to let loose before Mother died—big and full, starting from his stomach and working its way up. It was just like Wes laughed, I hadn't noticed that before, and now the two of them were laughing great and deep. The Ellie people were stomping and applauding. Cyril's face was curled up in pain. He fell to his knees: "No!"

"Oh, yes!" shouted Wes, slapping his thigh. "Rot'll do that. It's an awful bad thing!"

"Awful bad!" Dad yelped.

Yes, indeed. It was beautiful!

Gordon Mott grinned as Max and I rose to reach

our full agricultural potential. Click. Big Daddy lay at
our feet—soup and slop. Click. Mrs. McKenna shifted
like a queen who was losing control of her kingdom.
"There will be," she croaked, "a brief intermission
while we clean this . . . mess up."

Click.

But the crowd wasn't having any, and they weren't
going away. The sheriff dragged Cyril from the scale
as garbageman Pete Ninsenzo checked the damage. It
was great, wonderful damage—big, yucky, and deep.
Pete and two men carried what was left of Big Daddy's
shell away. The Rock River Volunteer Fire Department backed their truck in close and yanked out their
hoses. Nobody cared how long it took to clean the
mess up. It could have taken all night, all week, nobody was leaving.

The Ellie people started shouting my name. Phil
Urice gunned his truck into place as Cyril moved off in
agony.

"Ellie! Ellie!"

The Volunteer Fire Department hosed down the
area, and you couldn't tell there'd been a recent death
there at all, except for Cyril's wailing in the distance
and a few soaked streamers still hanging from the
scale. Mrs. McKenna's lips looked like they'd been
yanked tight with string. Mr. McKenna was chuckling
off by the 31 Flavors Harvest Turkey. Miss Moritz's
eyes were filled with the wisdom of history as she stood
arm in arm with General Patton sipping pumpkin
brandy in public below the scale where the great pumpkin Weigh-In winner was about to be announced to the
crowd who already knew.

Francis Lueking's pumpkin was shuffled on and off

like a bad act. "You did fine," she whispered to her squash. "It just wasn't our year."

It was my year!

"Number Ninety-six! Ellie Morgan!"

Nana hugged me hard. Wes helped me down from the truck like I was Cinderella. The Sweet Corn Coquettes lined up ready to shake my hand. I sucked in my stomach and tossed Mother's earrings. My eyes met Dad's, and our hearts knit together for all the world to see.

Foot-stomping and cheering people lined Marion Avenue underneath the hazy spotlights. A drumroll sounded. Mr. Soboleski blew his whistle. Dad, Wes, Richard, and Phil Urice marched forward to lift Max to victory. Mayor Clint rolled up his sleeves and grabbed a corner of Max's blanket to show he was a man of the people. The men shouted, "One, two, three," and hoisted Max like the true star he was onto the blanket.

"Ahhhhh," said the crowd as the blanket groaned under Max's humongous size. The men grunted and groaned and slid him onto the scale.

"Ohhhhhh," said the crowd.

"Six hundred eleven point seven pounds!" cried the weigher. "And solid, ladies and gentlemen. Through and through! We have ourselves a winner and a new Harvest Fair record!"

Yessirree!

There could have been a space shuttle launch right there on Marion Avenue and nobody would have noticed. The whoop that came from the people set the ground to moving. I jumped and raised my arms in victory. Orange confetti flew from hands like little butterflies. I hugged Max and took a bow.

Crash Bartwald and two defensive backs lifted me on their shoulders and paraded to the 31 Flavors Harvest Turkey, where the entire school gathered to show the adults where the real power in town was. Then everything started to blur. The clapping, the people. Dad waved from the crowd like I'd just been elected president. Wes stood with me. Richard jumped on a truck and made loud, immature sophomore noises. JoAnn and Grace threw confetti. The *Tribune* reporter asked me a question, and I couldn't think to answer. Justin asked how I felt about winning, which seemed really stupid, and I knew he'd make a great reporter someday.

People wanted me to say something, give a speech, make a comment, go on the record, be wonderful. But there was nothing to say because Max said it all. I was a grower and I'd done it. I'd killed myself trying and I didn't want to talk about it right now. I wanted to *feel* it, like a pumpkin soaks up the sun. I wanted it to be quiet, like it was in the patch, for just a moment. In the patch I could always catch my breath, I could always pick up the earth and let it run through my fingers. I could remember who I was.

Wes asked folks to back off real nicely. He put his hand around my shoulder and I leaned into him, glad for his protection. Max, the Biggest Pumpkin in Iowa, was covered with streamers and having a wonderful time. It was then that Wes leaned down and kissed me. Quick, you know. Not too dry or wet, but moist and full of promise—like good soil. My first kiss, with ninety million people watching, including my father and grandmother and loudmouthed cousin. I kissed him back and felt the sewers shake under Marion Avenue. We turned and faced the crowd, our couplehood sealed in front of the entire world—the Past President of the Gaithersville Ag Club and the Winner of the Rock River Harvest Fair and Pumpkin Weigh-In who had just set a festival record with a 611.7-pound giant, which also happened to be the greatest pumpkin in the world.

Who said agriculture is boring?

Chapter Sixteen

The blue ribbon Mrs. McKenna pinned on me was better than any of the blue ribbons she'd pinned on Cyril's smelly shirt for the past four years. Those were a wimpy shade of robin's egg blue, but mine was midnight blue, the color of a new Crayola crayon you'd use to color an important sky. The ribbon was long like a sash and had bright white letters. It read: 1ST PLACE, ROCK RIVER HARVEST FAIR AND PUMPKIN WEIGH-IN—GIANT PUMPKIN ADULT DIVISION, which, you've got to admit, is a terrific thing to say. At the bottom was a gold tassel that looked wonderfully official against my floppy orange blouse. Richard said I could probably rent a car with it even though I didn't have my license yet. Louise Carothers got measly second place and a short red ribbon with no character whatsoever and absolutely no tassel. I held my winner's check for $611.70—Max's weight at a dollar a pound. Frieda Johnson covered Max with a giant horseshoe wreath.

Wes put an orange derby hat over his stem, which made him look handsome and debonair.

Dad watched, beaming, his arm around Nana, waiting for me to reach my full potential and motivate the audience. Gordon Mott, the *Tribune* reporter, and Justin waited for my golden words.

I stepped to the microphone and said, "Thank you for believing in me and being my friends."

The people smiled at this and moved forward. They wanted more, and there wasn't any. Winston Churchill could have aced this gathering, General Patton would have whipped everyone into formation, but being a grower, I let my vegetable speak for himself. I stepped back as Max took center stage.

The sheriff was the first to shake my hand, and now I was shaking all the hands that shot my way. Dad jumped onstage and hugged me with total pride. Wes walked up, My Boyfriend, and hugged me with all the love in the universe. Mannie Plummer hugged Mayor Clint who she'd never voted for and probably never would. Jock Sudd shook Phil Urice's hand and Roxye snapped a picture of it in case they went back to hating each other in the morning. Spears tried to hug Aunt Peg and had to settle for a handshake. Grace hugged her mother, who hugged her happy Harvest hat because change comes hard to people of deep tradition.

Max soaked up the love like it was sunshine as Mother, Grandpa, and Bud DeWitt smiled down from Above.

Phil Urice's truck with me, Wes, Richard, and Max was moving down Marion Avenue for the four-block

Parade of Champions that nobody had turned out for during the past four years because who wanted to look at Cyril and his extreme grunginess shoving it in everyone's face so early in the morning? Roxye had decorated the truck with orange balloons and SQUASH 'EM, ELLIE! signs, and we rolled down Marion Avenue like returning astronauts from deep space who had captured the hearts of all America and who had done something magical and wonderful that everyone wanted to do, if everyone was being totally honest with themselves. I was waving and smiling, not like a Sweet Corn Coquette, mind you, but like a true growing champion. Richard was watching Wes and me closely with a look that said if we got cuddly, he'd jump out. Max stood tall and proud, the Biggest Pumpkin in Iowa, as the people heaped tons of confetti from rooftops and trees in celebration of our momentous victory over evil.

It was nothing, really.

Louise Carothers was behind me in her trailer with not near as many balloons or streamers. Gloria Shack looked like she'd bitten into a lemon. Mrs. McKenna rode in her carriage silent in the face of a new pumpkin phenomenon. Gordon Mott interviewed Dad about what kind of a child I was. Dad lied, which I really appreciated.

Mayor Clint called me "a rising Rock River star." The *Tribune* reporter interviewed me for forty-seven minutes and said I was the most determined teenager she'd ever met. Max was rolled back to his place near the big scale, where he would stay until Sunday afternoon, when the Rock River Pumpkin Weigh-In and Harvest Fair would be over.

I moved through the remaining festival days with the peace that comes from annihilating a despicable competitor. Wes was at my side. We shook hands with everyone. We smiled at children. We watched bakers stand beside their entries, swatting flies away, promising their husbands they would never do this again. Oral Perkins took a bite of Mannie Plummer's pumpkin fudge and started coughing, nearly finishing Mannie off right there. We kissed behind the pumpkin taffy poster and behind the 31 Flavors Harvest Turkey. I thought kissing was right up there with blue-ribbon-winning and figured anyone who got both would need a good rest before the week was out.

We rode in hayrides and bought lemonade from every kid who had a stand. We bet Richard two dollars that Bomber Urice, the three-hundred-pound favorite in the great pumpkin-pie-eating contest, would beat last year's record (seventeen) by two pies. He crashed to the ground after scarfing down his eighteenth pie. Richard stepped over Bomber's leg and took our money.

The fair surrounded us with big, loving arms. Storytellers told tales. Pigs snorted across Marion Avenue for the 3:00 P.M. races. Oratory contestants rolled good, rich words from their mouths. But nobody drew a crowd bigger than mine. When you've grown the biggest pumpkin in Iowa, people come. They just can't help themselves.

It was Sunday afternoon, and Max sat over his kingdom. In twenty minutes the festival would be over. I stood next to him in the winner's circle in my new turquoise jumpsuit (size 12), which had greatness written all over it, right down to the price, which made Dad gag.

Mannie Plummer stood next to me, a blue ribbon for "Best Pumpkin Confection" pinned to her dress. Frieda Johnson got "Best Overall Baking Category" for her cinnamon syrup buns, which didn't surprise anybody.

Gordon Mott ran out of things to say about pumpkins and the American spirit. 31 Flavors ran out of pumpkin swirl ice cream just in time, because everyone was getting sick of it. Bill Sudd ran out of customers, tipped back his hat, gazed into the sunset, and ran the Tilt-A-Whirl one last time.

The long shadows were forming on Marion Avenue—Mrs. McKenna's looked like a giant gourd, a clear sign the magic was going. She hoisted the Rock River flag with the dancing pumpkin insignia in a final blessing as Phil Urice unleashed the giant pumpkin balloon with the town motto—OUR PUMPKINS WE PRIZE/OUR RIGHTS WE WILL MAINTAIN—up, up into the air to fall to earth we knew not where. The crowd cried and hugged each other and made their plans for next year, which would be better than ever.

Winners grinned. Losers said they'd try again. And like a wonderful movie, it was over, leaving the spirit of its story behind. The people sighed and walked off arm in arm, turning back for one last look at Max, the Biggest Pumpkin in Iowa.

Max was loaded onto Phil Urice's truck, and Wes and I took him home. He went down with a thunk in his old place in the patch. Wes said he'd made pumpkins everywhere proud, which was absolutely true. But another truth was settling in, and I didn't want to think about it.

Max had only a few more weeks to live.

The days scrambled together. Max and I rode in the Homecoming Parade lead float under an orange banner that read NO GUTS. NO GLORY. This was a deep honor; even Richard said so. Max wore a Rock River High pennant taped to his stem, and I wore a defensive end's letter sweater that I had to give back to him after the game. Crash Bartwald jogged alongside in his football uniform, growling and spitting doom. We got devoured by the Ebberton Grizzlies, 21 to 3.

Halloween came, an awful holiday that insulted pumpkins everywhere—all those jack-o'-lanterns on doorsteps smiling like ghouls—any grower with a soul could see they were miserable. Richard came by on his way to Farley Raker's immature sophomore Halloween party dressed as the Gory Blob from the Cave of the Blood-Soaked Dead. He had worn out his Babe Ruth costume and was going for a new look with eyes all over his head and neck.

"Why," I shrieked, "can't people carve a face on a watermelon or a cantaloupe? Why torture pumpkins?"

"They're *harvest* vegetables."

"I can't have a conversation with you. You have fifty eyes."

"I have thirty-three eyes," Richard corrected. "Twenty-one more than Bart Tiller."

"What's he going as?"

"A mangy killer bat."

"He did that last year."

"Last year he was a depraved flying mammal."

"What's the difference?"

He raised his ketchup-stained sleeve: "A depraved flying mammal only has six eyes."

"I hate Halloween!"

Richard hissed and was gone.

The days grew dark and gray. Flowers disappeared. Trees stood bare and lonely. Marion Avenue was back to normal, even though it had felt the touch of greatness only a few weeks before. Wes and I were getting this kissing business down whenever possible, which meant when Richard wasn't around, but the hard truth of agricultural life pressed upon us. Max's shell was turning soft. My Vegetable was turning to mush. I knelt beside him in the patch.

"A pumpkin, Max, is not forever."

The ground was cold and ugly because it was November. It was going to be a long winter.

"I can't keep you much longer. You've got to understand."

I was rotten at explaining death to a vegetable, especially one as sensitive as him.

"Winter's coming."

Max stretched toward the sun. I patted him. "You can't hang on anymore. You're losing weight every day."

I hated November. It was dark and cold and mean even though it had Thanksgiving and all those pre-Christmas sales. I think the Pilgrims should have picked another month that made you feel more like celebrating.

I hated winter. It was a waste of time and talent. Barns closed, tools hung from hooks, unused. Tractors sat quiet and dusty. Soil froze solid, the sun stepped back, growers slept late and ate *brunch*. Everything stopped and waited for spring. I hated winter even more than Mayor Clint, who'd promised to keep Bud DeWitt Memorial Drive clear of snow, something old Mayor Bumper couldn't do, who said it was like trying to keep widows off an old bachelor. Mayor Bumper lost the widow vote that year, and everybody knows old bachelors are so cranky they don't vote. Mayor Clint won hands down, but folks were watching him real close.

Nana said winter was God's way of making growers catch their breath because the true ones would never do it on their own. She was right, too. If it were up to me, I'd be growing giants all year round, probably half dead from the strain and torture, gray before my time.

But Max didn't last until winter. One week before Thanksgiving, he knew it was time. I knelt in the dirt with Wes to say good-bye.

"I won't forget you, Max. You were the greatest squash in Iowa."

"The greatest," Wes agreed.

Max, a champion until the end, pushed up for one last reach to the sun. "I'll plant your seeds in the spring, Max. I promise." Wes held his stem. I took my cleaver and cut his flesh from top to bottom, again and again, until Max was a heap of chunks and muck. I was crying hard as we combed seeds from his insides and felt the pumpkin glop of an old friend run through my fingers—it ripped my heart, I can tell you—but it had to be done for the cycle to be completed. Max had seeds of greatness that money couldn't buy. Seeds that maybe could go the distance, like their father.

We lifted them carefully, knowing each one had a tiny embryonic plant inside filled with Max's spirit. We dried them and put them on a tray in the shed like they were gold, which they were. Then we cut Max's flesh and mashed it with corncobs and hay. Wes took a spade and I took one, too—we turned the earth over and over, and worked Max back into the soil where he had begun.

It was night before we finished.

We patted the last of Max into the earth. Wes stroked my hair, and warmth shot through me. I took a deep breath, a breath full of promise. I'd breathed it before as a grower lots of times—always when a squash relationship was over and a new one hadn't begun—always when I thought about spring, the time to till the soil of the last vegetable to make way for the new one. I held the tray of Max's seeds, thankful I could do the work I loved. Nana said life is a search to find who you are and who you aren't, and when you've found that, you've got one of God's best gifts.

This didn't mean I couldn't appreciate crossover potential. I did want to have great cheekbones and wear turquoise pants suits and have people notice when I walked into a room. I wanted Cyril to go to Russia and mine salt in Siberia where they weren't too keen on big-mouth competitors and a pumpkin would probably freeze the third week in August. I wanted to help Wes plant corn. I wanted to try to grow two giants next year, and I figured if that didn't finish me off, nothing would.

In a few months winter would be over and I'd be starting again. The Rock River would rise with pike, bluegill, and crappies, the roadsides would fill with marsh marigolds. The cottontail rabbits would hop around the new spring crop. I would bang a sauté pan good and loud to get them away from my pumpkins, scaring the robins who flew overhead. I would shout at the ground to stay warm *please*, is that too much to ask?

Spring would come like it always did.

It was one of those things you could count on.

Epilogue

By early April, Richard could do no wrong. He had hit two home runs and three singles in his past three games, nailed Billy Pike, Circleville's ace base stealer, for a double play, annihilating the Circleville High White Sox, 7 to 3, who absolutely deserved it, *and* caught a pop fly running into Howie Bucks, the left fielder, who was really ripped. Richard said this season had his name on it. He knew it back in February when Edgar, the Rock River groundhog, saw his shadow and we had an early thaw.

Edgar had been brought from the Northeast by Bob Robertson, who figured a Groundhog Day extravaganza would get folks pumped up about his newsstands. Some growers believed Edgar was one with the ground and could feel the warming of the soil from his hole below. I put as much stock in Edgar as I did in a fortune cookie. We were talking about a groundhog, after all—not a soil thermometer—an animal prone to a short life span for digging its home in stupid places, like under construction sites, and being mashed to death by giant cranes. If Edgar had been a dolphin or a Seeing Eye dog, I would have listened. These are animals that deserve respect. I was there when Edgar saw his shadow, and it wasn't much. Cyril clapped when Edgar came out of his hole. Dad called it "professional courtesy."

The fact that the Rock River started rising the next day just goes to show you how deeply every grower in the area needed spring. It came from nowhere, like a loon landing on a lake—making you wonder if it would float or sink. Flowers bloomed on hills and in gardens, willows sucked spring up their roots and grew full and proud. Windows flew open, screen doors got patched, growers took a great, healthy breath and started breaking up the ground—keeping their eye on the thermometer, because they'd been tricked before. Wes and I got his corn planted and told those shoots to push up toward heaven. He'd grown an inch since winter, which put the top of my head just below his chin. We were an agricultural couple of deep longevity now, and everybody respected it except Richard.

Dad brought out a new tape series that was becoming a hit. He called it, "Tilling the Soil of Your Mind's Motivation," and it was stuffed with deep agricultural truths for everyday living. We brainstormed on it together and had only one disagreement. I thought the tape should have a pumpkin patch on the label, *not* a field of wheat. Dad said pumpkins weren't mainstream motivational symbols, and I said he had the power to change all that. He decided not to. Dad gave me credit in the accompanying brochure, though, which was a great honor. I hung it on the refrigerator with a large pumpkin magnet.

Rumors were everywhere about Dennis and Ralphie. Judge Park made sure those boys understood the value of a pumpkin. Dennis was in a work-release program at the Circleville Pound—Grace heard he was cleaning the cages of rabid dogs. Ralphie was at military school—Richard said he saw him chained to other vicious teenagers, picking up cigarette butts along Route 7 with his teeth. I felt the judge was more than fair.

April 12 brought Cyril's annual Death Walk, which he took rain or shine, stopping at patches throughout the county, nosing around, giving the ground his nasty stare. Most growers put up with him, the way you'd listen to a life insurance salesman before you booted him out the door, except for Mannie Plummer, who shoved a rifle in his face and ordered him off her land. Mannie did this with life insurance salesmen, too. She decided long ago her life wasn't worth anything to anybody if she was dead and that when the time came, she was taking her money and her pumpkin fudge recipe with her.

Cyril stuck his rotten nose over my fence, which I'd been expecting. "Well, Missy," he sneered, "whatcha gonna have for the Weigh-In this year? Nuthin' much, I 'spect."

"You wish."

I was tilling the soil a secret way with the tiller Dad gave me for Christmas—in big circles the size of giant pumpkins to get it used to what was going to grow there. Tilling the soil is part of a grower's signature. I didn't want Cyril catching any of my secrets, so I said, "Come to see how we do it in the big leagues, Cyril?"

Cyril spat on *my* ground. A chipmunk would have

fainted from the fumes. He stared at me, and I stared back. This was a man who didn't deserve spring. All that beauty, all that freshness, all those splashes of color were wasted on him. We stared at each other for a while longer, which was really killing my mood. He walked away finally because there wasn't anything to say. There wouldn't be anything to say until August.

I had started my seedlings indoors in peat moss pots with sterilized potting soil. Frost could just sneak up on you without notice around here, and I wasn't about to stick sensitive seeds in the ground to have them wiped out overnight. Wes had been talking to Max's seeds all winter—speaking his heart out to them in the cold shed, where they were sealed up in a trash bag. You've got to be real sure of yourself as a person to pull this off. He was with me now, tucking seeds inside the pots, telling them about their daddy.

"Six hundred eleven point seven pounds, he was," Wes said. "Now which of you guys thinks you can beat the record?"

Dad wanted to have a seed planting party to applaud Max's seeds to victory, but I said it would be like inviting people along on your honeymoon. Some things need to be done in private.

I turned my grow light on the rows of little pots, keeping it six inches away to make sure the soil stayed at about eighty to eighty-five degrees—perfect for pumpkin growing. I had buckets of homework thanks to Miss Moritz, and did it at the kitchen table in case the seeds needed me. Miss Moritz had moved from World War II to Richard Nixon and the Watergate era. I was finishing my thousand-word essay "How Watergate Changed America and What It Means to Me and My Generation," building my thesis beautifully, I thought—how the seeds of Watergate injustice had been planted across the country and probably affected Dennis and Ralphie in their mothers' wombs (unless they were hatched), pushing them to lives of deep trickery and lonely exile. Miss Moritz wrote a note to Dad saying I related all important world events to pumpkins and that this could affect me later in life. Dad wrote back and said he'd gotten used to it.

Ten days after the little seeds had connected with peat moss, up came strong green sprouts—Max's kids! I was clucking at them, misting them with a gentle spray. They were beautiful. Soon the third leaf appeared on each one and we were ready to go outside and do what we had to do.

Wes and I loosened the soil in a twenty-foot circle to below one foot and conditioned the patch with composted cow manure, which was never a treat, but we were starting again, and I needed to get used to being miserable. Richard and Nana dragged a bag of genuine Morgan topsoil over from Nana's field, and we worked it into the ground, digging deep, feeling its magical powers take hold.

I waited and watered. Wes was watching his corn grow, and we worked together tending each other's fields, smelling springtime, and being in love. He'd given me his class ring, which clanged around my neck on a gold chain like a medal. It slammed Sharrell in the eye when she was wiggling down the up staircase and I was rushing up the *right* way. It left a small gash below her eyebrow. Nobody believed it was an accident.

The sun was good and strong, and my plants grew quickly. I watched the vines, letting only one pumpkin grow on each. I was checking day and night because we were entering into deep battle soon. The rule goes when you have a nice one the size of a soccer ball, pick off the rest and then kill yourself trying.

One pumpkin vine was different. It had a fruit the size of a watermelon. I didn't want to get too excited about this because it was still early in the season. Still, anything could happen, as we say in the growing biz. I knelt down in the dirt to make contact.

"Listen," I whispered. "I knew your father."

My pumpkin sat firm at this.

"I want you to start pushing out now. Pushing out good and strong, because you need to get tough. What we're about to go through is no picnic, believe me. You've never lived until you've made it through an ice storm in October." The pumpkin hung tough, which was a good sign he was champion material. Wes came by, and we sat with him for a while. I hadn't named this new vegetable yet. That came later, when we really got to know each other.

My dog, DeWitt, was barking at the raccoon that drove Mrs. Lemming crazy. Mrs. Lemming was back in town and leaving good garbage once again. DeWitt was still a puppy, not great to look at (low to the ground, short-matted brown-and-white fur), but he was everything you'd want in a pumpkin guard dog. He hated beef jerky.

"Good dog, DeWitt."

DeWitt crouched near the patch, sharpened his claws on a rock, and watched for predators. I was ready for anything this year and not taking any chances. You could never tell what heinous thieves might spring from the dust.

The Iowa sun crashed down like God was recharging the earth and flowed into my pumpkin who was stretching to reach his full agricultural potential. I leaned into Wes, running my fingers across the ground, and knew Max was in there as his boy pushed to grow from the soil that was full of his daddy.

It was perfect, that's all.

A perfect moment in agriculture.

Joan Bauer won the Delacorte Press Prize for a First Young Adult Novel for *Squashed*. She is a freelance writer who has worked in sales, advertising, radio, television, and film. She spent the first half of her career on the business side of both magazines and newspapers, the second half as a writer of screenplays and nonfiction. She was born in River Forest, Illinois, and now lives in Darien, Connecticut, with her husband, daughter, and assorted animals.